Reason and Reality

Lily is the Director of Student Activities at the University. She is single, young, energetic, exquisitely beautiful and in love with Samir — a bright and serious graduate student working for a doctoral degree in Astronomy and also the President of the Student Union. Samir is peculiarly intellectual, rational but emotional.

A unique feature Lily institutes at the University is that of "*Sunday Evening Forum*" presenting cultural programs, lectures and debates on topical subjects. Professor Henry Watson, a world-renowned authority on genomics, agrees to address the Forum on the much-sensationalized issue of human genetic engineering. Some find Dr. Watson's research on human cloning anti-God and Dr. Watson is blown off in suicide bombing. The suspects are indicted and a sensational trial held. Outraged at the culture of violence Lily runs for election to the legislature vowing to have a bill passed against public sale, possession and use of all kinds of firearms. Lily wins the election but big money lobby defeats her legislation. Lily resigns and embarks upon a "Recall Campaign" against the turncoat politicians. But then ...

MISHRILAL JAIN, *Ph.D., J.D.*, is an IP practicing attorney and a former professor of biology. He has authored several scientific and scholarly works, having also won a gold medal for a university world politics essay. His depth and fascination for exploring the essence of human culture, history and traditions while developing keen interest in the fundamental principles of natural sciences coupled with the incisive approach he had to develop for the practice of law, unavoidably thrust upon him an uncommonly analytical insight. *Reason and Reality* is his first novel, a unique fiction that flows through everyday life experiences touching various facets of modern human existence. It simultaneously touches the heart, haunts your thoughts, captivates your attention and brings you face to face to that universal truth, which is the essence of human spirit and experience. It is an uncommon literary fiction, which deeply and sensitively reflects multiple cross-currents shaping and influencing our lives philosophically, socially, politically and legally. It is an unusual novel of reason, romance and reality, passionately challenging, boldly honest and unerringly true.

Dr. Jain lives in the suburb of Baltimore, Maryland, U.S.A.
e-mail: mishrilaljain@hotmail.com

Reason and Reality

MISHRILAL JAIN

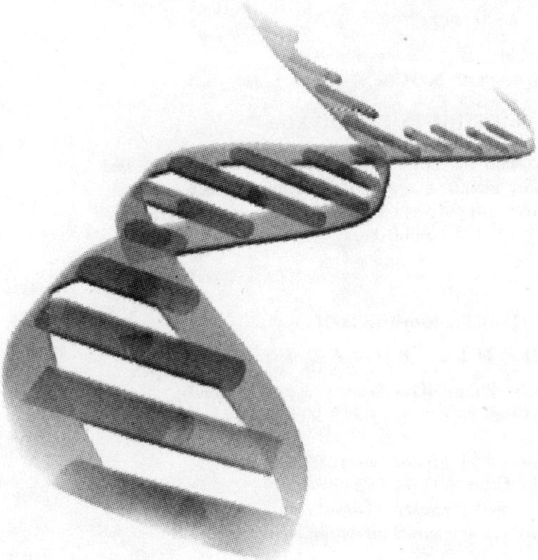

Academic Foundation
NEW DELHI

This novel is a work of fiction. Any reference to real people, events, locales, organizations and the like are intended only to give the fiction a sense of reality and authenticity. Other names, characters, places and incidents portrayed are either the product of author's imagination or are used fictionally.

First Published in 2004 by

ACADEMIC FOUNDATION

4772-73 / 23 Bharat Ram Road, (23 Ansari Road),
Darya Ganj, New Delhi - 110 002 (India).

Phones : +91-11-23245001, 02, 03, 04.
Fax : +91-11-23245005.
e-mail : academic@vsnl.com
www : academicfoundation.com

Reason and Reality
by Mishrilal Jain
ISBN 81-7188-351-6

Printed and bound in India.

Dedicated to

Kamal

who will never know
what she meant to me

Acknowledgments

My inexpressibly deep gratitude:

To Sudha Tewari who consistently stood by me to help make this publication possible.

To Rituraj Kapila of Academic Foundation who believed in my work and agreed to publish it.

To Ed Kurtz, my professor, who read every word of the manuscript and made corrections just as he did during my doctoral days.

To scholarly legal counsel Chittaranjan Nirmel for his praise and constructive critique of the manuscript both as a reader and a lawyer.

To my invaluably unique friend, Shanti Khinduka, who has the sharp wit and the sophistication of an academic for sharing with me his subtleties upon scrutinizing the novel.

To Surya Kaul for reading the draft of this book and providing invaluable comments.

And,

To those of my discerning colleagues who reviewed various parts of the story for factual accuracy, but who then collectively insisted to expressly dub this a 'fateful fiction', I do not know why!

Guarding the entrance to Heaven,
the Gatekeeper said to the visitor:
"Truth hurts. But if you don't,
Hell is where you will have to go."

... An anonymous Soothsayer

"Jinhen shak hai wo karen aur Khudaon ki talaash,
Ham to insaan ko duniya ka Khuda kahte hain."

... Ek Shaayar

1

"No Lily, no! You cannot proceed that way if you wish to win this election."

"Your reasoning may be quite correct but the reality is such that the people would simply not support your position and your opponent would surely paint you as some sort of a radical extremist. In politics, as in life, you cannot ignore reality and make decisions based on rationality alone," argued Samir embracing Lily.

"I love you Lily and I cannot let you assume undue risk for a cause that the majority is nowhere ready to accept," continued Samir looking deeply into Lily's eyes.

Lily didn't say anything and simply smiled.

It was a hot summer day and the sun, although a little bright, was just about ready to set. The mild orange-red glow of the setting sun had filled the clear sky and a cool breeze had begun to blow over the lake across Lily's house. The dusk was getting colorful with every passing moment and the reflective spectrum of the sky over the bouncing ripples made the lake look like a panoramic stage displaying the continually changing shades of the picturesque sky.

Lily loved the serene beauty of evening sunset and walked out of the house toward the lake holding Samir's hand. As she approached the lakeshore, she playfully began to run with her bare feet in the cool sandy lakeshore and teased Samir to catch her. Samir threw off his sandals and began to chase Lily. But Lily would dodge him with very swift movements, which made her long curly hair float in the breeze. As she suddenly stopped to change her course, the hair fell on her face and while she tried to push them back with the palm of her hand, she noticed Samir getting close and started running again.

They continued this playful touch and go for a while until the brilliant glow of the full moon emerged on the opposite side of the vast lake-spread. It was going to be a cozy moonlit night and they decided to leisurely stroll along the lakeshore till it was time for dinner, occasionally wetting their feet in the cool water, which seemed to instantly dissipate all fatigue. Mere touch of water felt so relaxing.

Lily was gorgeous and she looked dazzlingly beautiful under the radiant shadow of the moonlit sky.

Samir was extremely happy in her company.

2

It was getting late for dinner and Samir wanted to go home. But Lily insisted that he stay. "I have a lot of things weighing on my mind and I just need you to be with me,

Samir," said Lily while proceeding toward the kitchen. "But first tell me what would you like to have for dinner?" continued Lily opening the refrigerator.

"Don't worry, anything you have will do," said Samir while looking into the fridge.

"There are lettuce, cucumber, tomatoes, radish, and garbanzo beans. That will make some good salad," Lily suggested smilingly. "Then, over in the pantry, I am sure there is some minestrone soup, which I know you like. If I fixed some pasta with mushroom sauce, herbs and garlic, do you think that will satisfy you?" asked Lily, unable to hide the sweet sarcasm on her smiling face as she put some water in a pan for boiling the pasta.

"In fact, that sounds like a delicious dinner plan," responded Samir trying to find out everything stacked in the fridge. "I see that you have vanilla yogurt, fresh peaches and strawberries as well, perfect for dessert. I guess you knew what I can thrive on," happily remarked Samir who was always so fond of fruits and sweets.

"Lil, I tell you what! Why don't you go ahead and fix the pasta and I will prepare the salad," asserted Samir while taking out the vegetables from the fridge.

Lily took out the strainer, the cutting board, and the salad bowls, and set them on the kitchen counter. Samir tied the apron and began preparing the salad.

By now the moon had risen quite a ways above the

horizon and the clear sky was quite bright with twinkling stars. The dining room was contiguous with the kitchen and softly lit by the shining moon peeping through the skylights. Samir opened the windows to let the cool gentle breeze permeate.

Lily set the candles on the dining table and they sat down for dinner. Samir helped serving the meal.

Samir was an intellectual, analytic type and his scholarly studies of science and history of religion seemed to have made him an agnostic. It was not usual for Samir to say a prayer before the meal. But for some reason, perhaps sensing Lily's uneasiness from her insistence for him to stay this evening, Samir instinctively closed his eyes, folded his hands and began spontaneously: "O, mysterious force that endowed us with both, intellect and emotion, bestow upon us the courage of truth, the sanctity and eternity of love and the strength of character so that this life, which we must share, shall be ever humble and worthy of living. Amen!"

This was a bit unexpected, even surprising for Lily. And when they looked at each other, their eyes were a little misty with some sort of a fulfilling smile on their faces as they began the dinner.

After finishing the dinner Samir got up, came to Lily and helped her get off the chair. He then held her close by his arm over her shoulders and led her to step out on the deck open to the brilliance of the moonlit sky. Lily was speechlessly blushed being so proximate to Samir while walking out to the deck. She had never before felt Samir's touch so soothing, but being so shy she simply glanced intermittently into Samir's luminous soft eyes. Samir would only smile whenever Lil's eyes met his. It was apparent that her silent expressions revealed much more than what words could convey.

As they sat down on the bench under the soft glow of the twinkling stars, Samir found it to be the perfect moment for dessert. He got up, went in the kitchen, decorated the cool vanilla yogurt with fresh sliced peaches mixed with strawberries and brought out the dish to the deck table. He also had a little brown sugar on the side in case the fruits were a little tart. To Samir's taste, the brown sugar always added a little delight to vanilla yogurt mixed with fresh fruits.

Handing out the spoon to Lily, Samir gestured her to have the first bite of the dessert. Samir found this family tradition to be quite imaginative. But he noticed a bit of purposeful naughtiness in Lily's refusal. Samir was quick to respond. He held Lily by her arm, pulled her a little close to his side and touched her lips with the spoon full of dessert. Lily was throbbing pink with emotion. She looked at Samir, closed her eyes, and let him feed her the first scoop of the dessert he had so decoratively prepared.

Then she immediately grabbed the spoon, filled it with the dessert and fed it to Samir. They thus amused and entertained each other. But this did not subside the unease Lily was feeling inside.

Lily then got up and stood against Samir with her head on his broad shoulder; her arms wrapped round his chest. Samir gently touched Lily's chin and tenderly lifted her face so that he could unceasingly glance at the radiant beauty that Lily was! This caused a shivering sensation in Lily's entire body and in a soft subdued voice she murmured: "Samir, ever since you proposed that we serenade our love with matrimonial bond, I dream and think of nothing but you. It is unbearable that I cannot be united with you. Why must we wait, Samir?" Lily longingly looked at Samir with curious eyes.

"I know Lily this has been weighing heavy on your mind. But it has been difficult for me to persuade Papa to arrange our marriage. Had Mom been alive, it would have been easier. She was a woman worldly wise, practical, persuasive and understanding, all at the same time. Even in a man's world she knew how to influence decisions her own way. But you know Papa is conservative, traditional and obstinately conforming to the social norms. I have reasoned with him that the family must accept, and accept graciously, whomsoever I choose to love. But old traditions are hard to change and I am not sure whether reason would prevail over false pride. I know Lily how you must feel. I could fathom it the moment you asked me to stay with you this evening," Samir said with manifest agony.

"I did not want to leave any stone unturned if there was a way to pull the family together and avoid silly arguments, discord and resentments," Samir added merely as a reason and not as a justification.

"But I also know the futility of such efforts," Samir was pensive, adding: "I may have to defy the entire establishment, but Lil, no matter what the outcome, you shall always be mine and not even God could separate you from me," Samir was solemn as he held Lily close to his heart and gently kissed her forehead.

"No Samir, I will not let you struggle alone. I shall be with you every step of the way and nothing will keep us apart. It's just that sometimes the irreversible, unforgiving, incessant flow of time, which waits for nothing, bothers me and I want to be an inseparable part of you. Time gone is life lost, Samir. I do not know whether it says it all, but I just want every moment of my life merged into yours," said Lily as she embraced Samir with intense affection.

Samir couldn't help holding Lily into his folded arms as tears rolled over both of their determined but loving faces.

"Allow me to go home now, Lily. It's getting late and I had indicated to Papa that I would see him tonight.

Incidentally, pretty soon we must also plan our campaign strategy for your election to the parliament from the University precinct. Just relax, Lil. Everything will be fine. It will all work out."

And Samir wished goodnight to Lily.

3

As Samir left, Lily went straight to the open balcony upstairs and stood motionless against the parapet, her eyes fixed for a while at the serenity of the moonlit sky. The silence of the calm and quiet night was interrupted only by an occasional splash of the waves whenever a sudden gust of wind would sweep over the lake, and sometimes by repetitious chirping of crickets residing in the bushes and trees yonder.

A thousand thoughts were churning through Lily's mind and she began to pace slowly around the balcony deeply engaged in silent dialogue within herself, sometimes looking up, and sometimes looking down, as though carrying on some sort of a quiet conversation. "Whose business is it to decide how we must live and die? What values must govern individual decisions, social behavior and legal sanctions? And, simply because it is a democracy, must the majority always prevail over minority? And how does minority assert and achieve its legitimate rights without being frustrated by the majority? Why should every act of parliament assumed to be the right decision untainted by the influence of money and powerful interests? Samir is so faithful and honest, so innocent and devoted, so respectful and sincere of purpose, is it fair that his love must be tested by those who are nothing more than blind followers of tradition and orthodox faith? Why should the outdated and irrelevant social ethos prevail and dictate peoples' lives? Shouldn't the government's power be limited and people have the freedom of expression and choice?"— Lily was searching for answers to countless such questions that were agitating her mind.

Suddenly her thoughts were interrupted when the elderly housekeeper who had attended to her ever since she was a little girl, called on to remind her that it was almost midnight and she should be going to sleep. Lily smilingly nodded and requested "Baba" (as she lovingly addressed the fragile old man) to bring the folding cot to the balcony, for she felt tonight to be guarded by the twinkling eyes of the heavenly stars while the glorious moon looked on.

Baba brought a glass of warm milk mixed with a spoon of almond-saffron syrup, as Lily liked to have routinely before retiring. He fixed the bed for Lily and made sure that she covered herself with a shawl, for he felt it might get a little chilly during the night. He then tucked Lily into the bed (she was still a baby as far as Baba was concerned) gently arranging her silky hair that seemed a little tangled. Baba's loving hands somehow always made Lily feel so reassured and relaxed.

Baba then slowly stepped down the stairs to his quarters to retire for the night.

4

Lily's parents had acquired the house in which she lived. Her father was a high-ranking civil servant in the revenue and tax department of the government and all wealthy property owners and businessmen paid particular attention to his idiosyncrasies. He was invited to every function held at the city halls and clubs and expensive gifts were specially offered to his family whenever the "clients" (as they were called) could seize upon an opportune occasion.

Compared to the private sector, the pay scale in the civil service wasn't very attractive. But people pulled every string and brought every influence to bear to get selected into the civil service because, unlike the politicians who come and go, it was these officers who stayed and wielded the real power in the government. And, because of their "union," they couldn't be easily removed from their posts! This is what made the civil service an attractive career and these officials, who were supposed to serve the people, were indeed served *by* the people. And notwithstanding the power of politicians, these officials were recognized, pampered and treated as *de facto* authorities by shrewd businessmen who did everything possible to please them so that they could extract a favor when needed. They knew that there was always a loophole somewhere in the extensive, complicated tax and revenue code and there were no better persons to hint and suggest ways to benefit from these loopholes than these officials. Besides, one need not even hire an attorney to reap all the benefits and rewards of tax avoidance if one only knew how to tackle these bureaucrats! The businessmen were savvy enough to realize that any skillful experienced bureaucrat knew how to manipulate the system to assert his way and thwart the dictates of an adversarial politician boss.

Joseph Cohen was a prominent contractor-developer in the real estate business in this fast growing metropolis of Ocean City, where property values were skyrocketing due to the booming economy and increased demand for decent housing by continuous influx of employees. Apart from being the seat of the state capitol, the city offered all modern amenities including theaters, shopping malls, airport, railroad connections, university colleges, and hospitals. Above all, it had mild weather throughout the year and the lake and the ocean beaches were unpolluted. People enjoyed outdoor activities in all seasons. Moreover, for those who liked hiking and trekking, the mountain ranges were only a couple of hours away within easy driving distance. Real estate commanded premium price in this well planned growing city.

However, there were certain pockets in the city which were government properties and as was usually the case with public enterprises, they were unprofitable and a drag on the treasury. Joseph Cohen donated vast sums of soft money to the ruling political party, lavishly treated the influential politicians inviting them to stay at his exclusive ocean side resort, arranged fabulous parties for big bureaucrat bosses, and managed to obtain a long term (99 year) lease to build and develop one of such properties. It was through such wheeling-dealing and wining-dining that Joseph Cohen made millions, spent millions, and in return made many more millions. He was a master of working the system and always careful not to ruffle any feathers of government authorities. Indeed, ever so cleverly Joe tried to boost the super ego of public officials and made them feel important in a subtle manner. But he also recognized the innate desire of humans to have all the material comforts of life, which these civil servants could not afford with their fixed and limited salaries. Joseph was most adept in accomplishing all of this without any appearance of impropriety.

Suzanne Cohen, Joseph's wife, was an equally sophisticated and gracious lady. She was meticulous about every little detail from Hors D'oeuvres to all cuisine, entrees, wines, drinks, and desserts, and made sure that all attendants serving the parties were smartly dressed, polite, courteous, and quick. Even though paid only the minimum wages, these attendants nevertheless felt lucky that they got hired to serve Cohens' parties.

Suzanne always made it a point of personally greeting the wife of every dignitary at the party and conversing with them with great affection and niceties so as to make them feel at home as though she were the closest friend they had.

A live band played favorite tunes at these gala affairs and people drank and danced feeling happy, romantic, and gleeful under the soft glow of marvelous chandeliers, picking up an assortment of sweets from the dessert tables arranged all around the dancing floor whenever there was a slight pause for the band leader to introduce a new tune.

These parties concluded with a big toast and as the guests slowly dispersed, the Cohens accompanied every guest to their car to bid them goodnight and Suzanne made sure to leave a beautifully wrapped gift box in the back seat of the car. Some of Cohens' friends were famous jewelers and the Cohens had delicate but elegant gold, diamond and other precious stone jewelry of all kinds (necklaces, earrings, bracelets, tie pins, shirt buttons, cuff-links, etc.) tastefully prepared for presenting as gifts. Of course, the guests would express hesitation and remark: "You didn't need to do this, Suzie" to which she would simply say: "O, this is nothing! Only a small token of appreciation. I hope you like it." And the car moved as Suzie closed the door.

Joseph Cohen was most grateful to Lily's father for being so pivotal in arranging the long-term lease for developing the government property. It was a multimillion dollar project and he stood to gain handsomely from this deal. Lily's father had only casually mentioned his desire to have a retirement home near the lake, but as perceptive as Joe was, he understood what was meant and thought it was a small price to pay. Indeed, he considered it a good business investment if he obliged Lily's father with his desire of having a retirement home become a reality.

Joe was quite calculating and recognized the value and importance of the right time, right place, right occasion and right opportunity. He immediately looked up the area's site plan, selected the best possible lot closest to the University with an excellent view of the lake and had a beautiful house built on it. He then recorded the deed in Lily's name. Lily was quite young then, and her parents still lived in the housing provided by the government for high-ranking officials. Lily's father was overwhelmed with Joe's generosity and although he did not overtly express anything, deep down he felt the magnanimity of Joe's benevolence and didn't know how he would ever be able to repay such a splendid favor.

Since the house was within walking distance of the University, Lily's father arranged for Lily to use this house from the time she enrolled in the University; her parents visiting often, particularly over weekends.

Lily's father still had a few years to go before retirement and Joe was quite assured in the knowledge that the favor done will multiply in many favors returned.

5

Although the University was an Ivy League private institution where admission requirements and fees both were very high, somehow the kids of very famous and rich, particularly the children of heads of government of foreign countries, managed to get admitted regardless of their academic record. Perhaps the presence of these kids of the high and mighty added to the prestige and recognition of the University, at least that was the perception.

Unless substantial savings were made, meeting the high cost of college education at these private prestigious institutions was generally prohibitive for the wards of median income families despite much publicized scholarships, student loans and the availability of other forms of financial aid. And even if they succeeded in obtaining financial aid, the burden of repayment of the accumulated loan with interest dissuaded many a young college-bound student from enrolling in these high-cost schools. And among those who were motivated and ambitious enough to graduate from these schools, many delayed getting married and raising a family until they felt financially secure to afford it. They were quite well aware that financial stress and arguments over money were a major cause of family breakdown and divorce. Hence, either out of necessity or of choice, living together without getting encumbered with the marital obligations and limitations seemed preferable to this young generation. After all, they reasoned, why think of marriage until raising children was a definitive consideration? The society may not approve of sexual relationship outside marriage, but who cares? Two consenting adults could engage in whatever type of relationship they wanted and many a parent during their heydays had pre-marital sex anyway. So, 'what have they got to complain about?' — was the generally prevalent argument.

Everyone wanted to send their kids to the college. People recognized the simple fact of life that money mattered more than morality and in this age of competitive global economy where financial advantage was contingent upon technology-driven trade and commerce, earning depended on learning. College education seemed to be the key to economic success and financial security. However, the conservative parents worried that once in the college, the kids act liberated and independent. The dormitories, fraternities and sororities all had fun during the freshman year and some indulgence in alcohol, some sex and some experimenting with drugs were all expected, though not wished, and certainly not endorsed. For these college kids virginity was not a virtue. It was simply a hypocritical denial of biological reality. At least for those who thus argued, seeking pleasure, fun and enjoyment was not a sign of moral decay; it was simply a part of living a happy life. "To hell with those who believed otherwise," they would say. True, the universities were great seats of education and learning on which careers and progress depended, but they were also a liberating force that naturally grew out of knowledge, intellectual inquiry, independent thinking and freedom of association, at least that is how things appeared to be.

Samir was a bright and serious graduate student working for a doctoral degree in the Department of Astronomy at the University. He was one of those few whose outstanding scholastic performance won him full graduate tuition scholarship and a fellowship to pursue higher education. He was quite sociable but also well aware of the self-indulgent, pleasure seeking instantaneous gratification ethos of the student crowd and did not want any part of it! So he opted to stay by himself in a rented room close to the University. Daily commute from home was neither feasible nor practical.

But Samir was mature enough to realize the realities of the times and of the trends. He neither criticized nor abhorred the student body. He recognized that each and everyone must reason for itself as to what was right and wrong and despite individual freedom, there could also be collective consciousness, common cause and unity in diversity. This frame of mind rendered him a natural leader; tolerant, non-dogmatic and a consensus builder. He was an amiable cohesive force. For these qualities, he was much liked by fellow students and was elected president of the student body.

The University had an undergraduate enrollment of more than 30,000 and the student body was quite active in policy matters. Samir was very respectful of the faculty advisory committee and he made sure that all deliberations, discussions or debates were carried out with decorum, dignity, politeness and respect due the advising professors. Samir's objective, thoughtful discourse and mature mannerism fostered a cordial relationship between the administration and the student body and earned him an influential role in university affairs.

6

Samir's contact with Lily came about because of her position as the Director of Student Activities at the University. It was an unavoidable interaction because Lily had to coordinate the social activities in concert with the student body schedules. Hence, she had to get together with Samir in his capacity as the president of the student body to discuss the plans, programs, activities and the calendar on a continual basis.

Having completed a graduate program *suma cum laude* in the School of Social Work and having earned a Master's degree with a minor in Political Science, Lily had joined the University as the Director of Student Activities. She had a uniquely accommodative attitude, attractive demeanor and outgoing personality. She was young, energetic and exquisitely beautiful with a pleasant innocent smile flashing over her tall charming body, so much so that sometimes when she would pass by a batch of athletes playing around on the campus, some would whistle at her to which she did not take offence, rather responded with a waving hand and it all cooled down in great fun! She knew that physical attraction is paramount in human eyes and men adored women of beauty. But she was self-assured, confident and secure within herself, which was a source of great strength and of uninhibited easy exchange with people.

A unique feature Lily instituted at the University was that of "Sunday Evening Forum" under which on the last Sunday of every month, a special program open to all in the community was sponsored under the aegis of the University. The program presented lectures and debates by recognized authorities on topical subjects, award winning operas and musical concerts, foreign acclaimed documentaries or movies and other cultural performances by outstanding artists. The quality, selection, and organization of Sunday Forum became very popular and endeared the audience so very much that as soon as Lily entered the huge hall to introduce the program and welcome the guests, a thunderous applause greeted this intelligent youthful lady of style and grace. Lily's modest and easy accessible nature added to her popularity and recognition throughout the University and the community. Samir was quite instrumental in organizing and arranging the programs and the success of Sunday Forum deepened Lily's dependence on Samir and they began to discover each other's feelings as they worked closely together.

◆ 7 ◆

Being a student of astronomy, Samir's subject matter related to the study of stars, to unraveling the mysteries of the cosmos, to finding that unifying physical law which governed all forces and relationships between matter, energy, space and time, and explaining the origin and destiny of the universe wherein humans appeared to be an incidental evolutionary phenomenon. Or, were there order, design and purpose in the seemingly entropic "Nature," Samir would sometimes wonder?

Astrophysics and mathematical proofs within the framework of relativity and quantum mechanics fascinated Samir. In the final analysis, he realized, all theories and observations had to be reconciled with mathematical congruities within the laws of physics, which seemed to apply to all known phenomena. But he also recognized that there was always room to challenge the established theories and propose fresh ideas with new mathematical models. For science never claimed finality to any theory. It only provided a systematic method and process for finding answers. While abstract logic and conceptual beliefs may propose answers to questions, it was rigorous testing and unfettered questioning of answers that was the essence of science and epistemology, Samir posited. Therefore, he would let his mind float free almost to the boundary of philosophy, but the rigors of mathematics and the requirement of proofs soon brought it all down from the abstract to the realm of reality.

When, where and how did all this begin? Were time, space, motion and all else non-existent as separate entities before the 'Big Bang' and came into being only thereafter? If so, what was the nature and origin of that 'Singularity'? How did gravitational force that seems to invisibly influence, if not regulate the motion, the geometry and all else in the universe, then originate? If there is an equal and opposite force to every acting force and if there is 'matter asymmetry', is there another universe where antimatter and antiparticles predominate? Or, must there be other universes?

Every answer seems to raise new questions. Is there a reason why there must be an ultimate answer to all questions? Must there be a universal cause to all effects? Or, are there certain unknowable uncertainties that shall remain indeterminable? And is this where philosophy and religion come into being? Is this where faith and belief supplant reason and reality, even if the premises of philosophy and the beliefs of religion were incongruent, nonconforming or contrary to the fundamentals of physical sciences? Is it metaphysics that ultimately rescues the limitations of human reasoning and rationality?

Samir would think aloud posing such questions and exploring various paradigms with Lily on his way to the astronomical observatory to collect data being recorded by all sorts of computerized instruments including powerful orbital telescopes, radio wave and X-ray detectors, infrared satellite cameras, spectrographs and other such analytical tools. Lily would insist on accompanying Samir to the mountain top observatory, for she was intrigued by what the telescopes and the instruments reveal about the 'heavenly bodies'. She was awe struck seeing through the telescope the ridges and craters on the moon, the spiraling nebulae and the rings around Saturn! She was fascinated how the invention of the telescope had expanded the frontiers of human knowledge and discovery of cosmic phenomena. Samir and Lily both thought that the observation of other stars having planets circling around them similar to those in the solar system was an exciting discovery and as Samir discussed certain aspects of his planetary studies, Lily marveled at the imagination and accomplishments of human ingenuity. The more she learned about Samir's thesis, the more she adored him and Samir loved Lily for her understanding and support. And before leaving the observatory, Samir would take Lily to the observation deck outside the instrument room where both of them would look together at the twinkling heavens above.

Neither of them knew how emotions evolved and why

love transcended reason.

They just felt inseparable from each other.

8

The more Lily witnessed Samir's total absorption in the mathematical formulations related to his studies, the more Lily realized the magic of mathematics and understood the curiosity-seeking dimension of human endeavor which propelled them to painstaking pursuit of knowledge for its own sake. Nonetheless, Lily thought that the issues facing humanity on this Earth were no less daunting. The economic disparities, the unchecked greed-laden profit motive, the socio-political spins and intrigues, the manipulation of public opinion and the power plays of money appeared to pervade every facet of life. Earning a living, keeping a job to raise a family and planning for retirement seemed to preoccupy and govern people's lives more than the esoteric issues of ethics, morality, heaven and hell. However, the discovery of pluripotent embryonic stem cells, genetic and tissue engineering, new techniques of controlling human reproduction, advanced medical and surgical procedures, computerized nanotechnology and decoding the DNA sequence of the human genome provided an unprecedented outlook on human destiny. Lily found these issues affecting human existence, experience, achievement and quality of life quite challenging as she shared her feelings with Samir.

Samir appreciated and fully understood Lily's views and readily acknowledged that there was another dimension to the earthly reality apart from seeking the reason for its existence. And, with that realization he said to her: "You know Lil, with a single minded focus on my studies of cosmic existence, I often lose sight of the realities of earthly existence. I get so engrossed in my own mental universe that during those moments the whole world appears to become non-existent for me! It may seem strange, but while working out the complex mathematical relationships, I get so thrilled, so excited and so carried away with immense joy that nothing else seems to matter. I do not know how to say it Lily, but your concern for human condition, your realism, objectivity and pragmatism, your sense of here and now, fills a void in my life. You are just what I need, but do not have! Do you think I could ask you to be a part of me, Lily?"

Samir looked into Lily's soft emerald eyes as he spoke those words.

Lily didn't know what to say but simply asked: "Do you think you can handle me?" to which Samir retorted while embracing her: "Are you sure you can handle me...e...e?" And they both remained embraced with each other until Samir softly whispered, "I love you Lily and you will be dearer to me more than my own life."

Lily was overwhelmed and tears rolled down her happy face.

Samir was full of emotion and wished to celebrate this memorable event in his life. And he wanted to do so befittingly. But he did not wish to reveal his mind and wanted a total surprise on Lily. Suspense and anticipation, he thought, will be more fun and even more exciting. So he lightheartedly proposed that he will quickly finish up some of the work he had to complete at the University and wondered if Lily could spare the weekend for him. Lily didn't quite understand what Samir was up to, but she said: "Only on one condition, Samir. You will have to do what I wanted you to do. No excuses!"

They both seemed a bit mischievous, but they were ready, rather eager for the weekend.

A mysterious sense of excited anticipation appeared to have pervaded both of them.

9

As Lily returned home she couldn't believe what had occurred! How, without any inkling, without any notion, entirely unbeknownst, Samir became inseparable from her and she formed a part of him! Is this how love just happens? Is this how feelings just spring? Is it so magical that love cannot be explained, just experienced? Just felt? Lily didn't understand anything. She was simply so happy, so ecstatic that she didn't care to bother her head with anything else and let it all remain as mystical and mysterious as it may.

Lily wished to relate all of this to her parents but on second thought she hesitated. For she knew that in her parents' view so called "love" was merely a romantic idealism, an emotional involvement of youthful imagination and an infatuation of weak moments. Once the lovey-dovey phase subsides and the passion dissipates, the contentions, conflicts and clashes begin to test the patience and tolerance, they thought. And unless there was an abiding faith rooted in loyal commitment in the form of unbreakable matrimonial bond, not always an easy accomplishment, the realities of life quickly replace "love", they often expressed.

Lily didn't wish to ruin her happiness getting into an argument with her parents. Hence, she simply decided to skip mentioning anything to them and related all that had happened to her dear old Baba, whose only happiness was to see Lily happy. All other worldly considerations and contentions were beyond Baba's worries. Hearing all that she had to say and seeing Lily exuberant with a sweet smile on her face, Baba instantly hugged her and after a brief pause, thoughtfully said: "This is an auspicious occurrence and a monumental moment in your life and I wish my Lily all the joy and happiness in the whole world."

Lily again didn't understand anything. She just kissed Baba on his gentle hands and got ready to retire for the night.

But Lily couldn't fall asleep. Although she didn't believe in mysticism, she wanted to figure out what Baba meant? More importantly, she began to make plans how she would "handle" Samir, where would the honeymoon be, what she wanted to accomplish together with Samir, and everything else that a bride-to-be gets excited about. Thinking of such things she fell asleep.

But Lily woke up several times during the night perhaps dreaming dreams. She still seemed excited and it was mysterious how her thoughts would continue into the dreams. But when she woke up she was smiling and energetic, though still incredulous as to what had happened.

Samir called ahead of time to make sure that Lily was ready when he arrived to pick her up first thing on Saturday morning.

He had planned precisely how he wanted to commemorate the day with Lily.

10

The predawn sky was beautiful and the birds had started landing on the porch. Lily took shower, neatly arranged her hair and put on her most elegant new dress imprinted with light pink flowers on mustard yellow silk satin. She wanted to look her best for this first meeting after Samir proposed to her. The dress was a perfect fit on Lily's young body. She was quite conscious of her femininity, which made her a bit shy, but she was also uninhibited about her attractive features. She was restless in anticipation of Samir's arrival to pick her up. She had Baba prepare the special sweet dish that Lily knew Samir fondly enjoyed and had Darjeeling tea and breakfast ready to share with Samir.

Though intellectual by nature, Samir was quite sensitive and imaginative. He thought that Devon Square on the west side of the town was a fascinating place with unusual ethnic boutiques, shops and restaurants which were open over the weekend, not too far to drive and Lily would be absolutely enchanted by out-of-this-world ethnic experience. Samir had planned precisely how he wanted to treat Lily and he was impatient for the celebration he had discretely arranged for the evening, although he didn't mention anything to Lily.

Samir couldn't take his eyes off Lily's stunning beauty as she opened the door for him to come in. Unable to resist his feelings but being restrained by his own shyness, Samir was momentarily hesitant but managed to meet Lily's bashful eyes as he proceeded toward the family room where breakfast was arranged. Blessing affectionately, Baba hugged both within his folded arms and insisted on allowing to serve them breakfast with his own hands.

Somehow these old folks felt a fulfilling sense of joy and seemed to derive particular pleasure from preparing something special and serving their loved ones with their own hands! Though fragile due to age, Baba nevertheless appeared quite energetic this morning and had a peculiar sense of satisfaction in his eyes as he served breakfast to Lily and Samir.

After finishing breakfast, Samir escorted Lily to the car and proceeded to the destination he had preplanned.

It was a very pleasant morning. There were only a few thin scattered clouds in the sky allowing the sun to peep through intermittently. The weather was delightfully mild and Samir kept the car windows open. The air was fresh and the roadside trees and meadows were lively. Along the drive, the thick bright yellow patches of buttercup flowers sprinkled hither and thither over the luscious meadows made it appear as if a vast green carpet with an embossed golden design had been rolled out over the entire landscape. The wide-open stretch of the meadows was serene and delightfully soothing to the eyes.

"It is beautiful out here, Samir. It makes me wonder why people don't come out of their apartment life and camp out under nature's bounty? Anyhow, where are we headed to, Samir?" asked Lily. Not being so crazy about driving, Lily had not been on the road very much and didn't know various destinations outside the city.

"Yes, it is gorgeous on this terrain and it certainly would be fun to camp out here. But, it is even better on the other side of the mountain range opposite the observatory where the river bends overlooking the plain," Samir explained. "You can't see it all very well from the observation deck without the binoculars or viewing telescope. But it is so colorful and majestic, particularly when all hues of flowers are in full bloom."

"Have you been there before?"

"Only a couple of times, but it is so different each time! Nature prefers to have its own secret design for displaying its grandeur, it seems".

"How far is it from here?"

"About an hour and a half. But that's not where we are going right now."

"We aren't? So where are we going?"

"Remember, you are mine and I had you spare this weekend for me?"

"And remember, you agreed to do whatever I asked you to do?"

"A deal is a deal. I shall live up to it."

"So shall I."

And they thus teased and cajoled each other on the way.

The cool morning ride in the car was delightfully invigorating.

11

Soon, much to Lily's surprise, Samir pulled the car over on a flat plateau from where the riverbank was easily approachable by trekking through the flower-laden meadow. Samir selected this spot purposefully, for he wanted Lily to walk through the meadow touching and feeling the beauty of those red, blue, yellow and purple flowers scattered all over that gorgeous patch of landscape. And as Lily was stepping out of the car, he took out from the trunk a bag full of clothes, towels, water proof sandals and other necessities and handing it over to Lily he said: "Here Lil, this has everything I think you'll need to change for white-water rafting down the river about a quarter mile away. It will be fun and I am sure you will enjoy it."

"But I have never done white-water rafting."

"Well, that's the whole point. Something new and

exciting that you will never forget!"

Lily didn't say anything, just looked into Samir's mischievous eyes and smiled.

It was not a commercial outfit. However, the private park service had the rafting facility exclusively for the observatory staff and provided the inflatable rubber boat, paddles and lifejacket. A guard was on duty for help if needed.

There were several other groups of observatory staff assembled also for white-water rafting, which was scheduled to begin around noon and everyone was supposed to return by no later than 4 p.m. Although the river stretch for rafting did not require that much time, people often stopped by at certain spots for picnicking or hiking or simply to rest and enjoy the natural beauty of the valley before concluding the trip.

All of this caught Lily a bit unawares, but she was fascinated by the awesome splendor of the valley as she walked down the path toward the rafting station. She then took the bag Samir had pulled out of the car trunk for changing in the stall at the rafting station, all the while bemused at figuring out how Samir may have managed to pick out the comfortable style and proper size of the swim suit and all other items, including a casual dress to wear after rafting, sandals, a pair of underclothes, a mirror, hair brush, etc. And, she was tickled at mere thought of Samir's fancy while changing into the swimsuit. Meanwhile Samir quickly got ready for rafting by putting on his swimming trunk. He felt invigorated with the touch of warm air over his bare chest. He picked up the water bottle and a watertight packet containing sandwiches, snacks and fruits, which he had brought along with him.

Having enjoyed a couple of times before, Samir found white-water rafting quite thrilling and he was perfectly comfortable at it. But this was Lily's first encounter and she had no clue what to expect, although she was quite excited about it. As all others began to pull their boats on to the water, Samir pulled his rubber boat out far enough on the water so that it floated freely and asked Lily to get in as he held the boat stationary. No sooner did Lily step in the water than she exclaimed: "O my God, it's cold!" But then, as if to hide her embarrassment, she immediately said "O, but it feels good in this warm weather," and she cautiously managed to get into the boat which wobbled a little making her a bit nervous while trying to put her foot inside the boat. As she was trying to get situated in the boat, Samir asked her to sit in the middle and hold the paddles while he pushed the boat farther down the stream and jumped in the boat. He then took over the paddles from Lily and began to propel the boat so as to take it mid stream down the river's flow. There were some boats ahead and some behind him and they were all talking in loud excitement, mostly instructing each other how to maneuver the boat in the right direction.

The sun had risen overhead in mid sky, but the cast of thin clouds kept the temperature warm without getting too hot. The clear refreshing water in the pristine river was just about knee deep on this stretch, getting deeper where the riverbed sloped at the rapids. Nevertheless, even at the rapids the fine pebbles on the riverbed were visible through the clear water so that if someone failed to control the boat at these rapids, they could safely land on the riverbed or swim and grab the boat and resume the fun at the next rapid. Occasionally, some boats would get stuck on sizable rocks along the river bends, requiring the occupants to get out of the boat into the water and push the boat out over the flow and resume paddling.

Lily intently watched how easily Samir stroked the water with the paddle and how he steered the boat in a particular direction and soon she was anxious to paddle the boat herself.

"Go ahead, grab the other paddle and try," said Samir.

"It's easy, it's fun," said Lily as she began paddling the boat. Samir helped now and then with his paddle whenever the boat seemed to go off course, until the boat reached a fast rapid at a river bend. Samir knew that this was the most exciting part of rafting and he wanted Lily to handle the sturdy but flexible rubber boat in whatever manner she could and experience the thrill.

The boat dipped and swirled with speed as it hit the swift rapid with a big splash of water soaking Lily and she screamed "O my God, we are going to sink!" but by the time she caught her breath, the boat had passed the rapid and Samir was smiling at Lily while trying to steer the boat away from the bend toward midstream again.

"You know, you are so naughty, Samir. It was so scary! And, with that big splash of cold water suddenly coming all over you, you feel as if you were going to drown!"

"But you didn't. Did you? Only the heart may have stopped throbbing for a moment, but that's the thrill."

"Wow, it seems we are coming soon to the next rapid. But I am all set now. I am going to have lots of fun with this one, now that I know what to expect," and Lily took the paddle again and began steering the boat.

The second rapid was a little more stretched and the boat dipped and swirled several times with waves splashing directly over Lily's face, soaking her wet all over while she was trying to control the boat to no avail. Samir was relaxed and watched Lily's nervous struggle with great fun, being confident of his skills to steer the boat to the riverbank after passing the rapid.

"Wasn't that fun?" asked Samir as he took over the paddle to propel the boat toward the river bank where he wanted to dock, for he thought it was high time to have something to eat.

"My, O my! It sure was fun, but boy it was still scary, I must admit."

"I knew you would savor this experience."

"Well, it sure will remain etched in my memory indelibly. But, you are wicked, aren't you?"

"You ain't seen nothing yet, Ma'am," and so saying Samir pulled the boat up on the riverbank and asked Lily to come out. Lily had no problem now to quickly get out of the boat.

Splashing river water didn't bother her any more.

12

It was partly cloudy and the warm sun felt soothing on the wet body. Lily preferred a picnic bench under the partial shadow of a tree, one-half of the bench being in the shade and the other half being in the sun. Samir laid open the food bag and let Lily choose whatever she wanted from the assortment of veggie sandwiches, cheeses, Doritos, bananas, plums and biscuits, etc., he had packed.

The wetness of the swimsuit made it adhere to the contours of the body and as Lily sat under the sun, the dark nipples of her firm conical breasts seemed to become apparent making her self-conscious and bashful fearing that

Samir would notice them. But she was helpless and tried to hide her consciousness by asking Samir to open the water bottle while she concentrated on the food. Samir was sitting on the other side of the picnic table from where only Lily's long curly hair were visible with a few water droplets glistening under the sunshine.

Samir was hungry and quickly finished eating. He then turned toward Lily and asked her if he could squeeze the water out of her dripping long hair so that she could neatly tie them back again. Lily simply looked at Samir and nodded with a sweet smile. Samir's mere touch of her silky hair seemed to send a shiver through Lily's spine and as his fingers softly glided through her hair, she sighed: "O, Samir!"

Samir felt Lily's emotions and whispered softly: "I adore you Lily and I do not know how to express it adequately but you are all that I want in my life, my dream come true."

There was still something within Lily, she didn't know exactly what, that felt unfulfilled as she looked at Samir's tall, handsome, muscular body which she couldn't resist embracing as she mumbled without knowing what else to say: "Samir, I love you."

"I love you more than you can imagine" Samir whispered as he felt the sensation of Lily's full breasts touching against his bare chest. But Samir didn't want to embarrass Lily and quickly added, “I think it’s getting time to go back, for we still have to reach the terminal point where the boat has to be returned. Do you want anything else from the food bag or should I dispose it off?”

“No, I had plenty. I only need a sip of water. That’s all.”

“Come with me for a moment, though. Look at that hill covered with those flowers dancing with the breeze. I think you wouldn’t want to miss seeing the valley from that vantage” suggested Samir.

Lily couldn’t wait and as was typical of her, she began to run up the hill to reach there first. Samir followed behind, on purpose not to take her over.

“See, I beat you” declared Lily triumphantly as she reached the high plateau. “Good Heavens! What a view this is! Look at those tall lively oaks, the red robins, the finches, the flirting butterflies and the weeping willows kissing the silently flowing river. Ah, it’s so majestic, so awesome!”

“It was equally magnificent when I was here the last time.”

“It’s just so beautiful, so unforgettable. But we must get back now. Right?”

“I guess so.”

And they returned to the boat and resumed rafting, Lily paddling all the way and enjoying every moment of it.

13

After returning the boat, Lily changed into the casual but graceful silk dress Samir had brought, arranged her hair into two stylish braids which reached down beyond the back of her shoulders and put on the soft leather sandals Samir had picked. Lily's features were so very attractive that no matter how she made her hair, she appeared most magnetic. And, with a sweet smile, which could only be expressive of deep feelings within, she looked irresistibly charming to Samir as she walked back to the car. Opening the door for Lily to get in, Samir softly kissed her while she was entering the car. He then headed on to the road westward.

It was still about an hour before sunset and Samir was quite confident of reaching Devon Square on time. But again, Lily had no clue and Samir wouldn't give any hint when asked: "What's your plan this time, Samir?" to which he smilingly answered: "We have to have dinner, don't we? And that's where we are going."

"O, Ya?"

"Yes, indeed."

"What kind of food?"

"Oh, it's a restaurant which will prepare any kind of dish you like. But, it prepares them in Tandoor. You know what that is, don't you?"

"No, I don't have the foggiest idea."

"Well, it's an ancient clay oven designed in such a manner that it bakes the food in an even temperature and the Tandoori recipes are so delectable that you just have to taste them to appreciate the unique flavor and quality of the preparation. And the Tandoori bread or Nan when it comes out of the oven is so tender and delicious that I am unable to describe it's delicacy. You just have to try it out yourself."

"Looks like I am headed for another experience this evening."

"That's for sure."

"You are too much, Samir."

"Well, I don' know about that but we will soon find out."

"But where is this restaurant?"

"In Devon Square."

"Never heard of it."

"That's because you don't venture to explore the other worlds out there, I guess. There is so much to experience, enjoy and discover if we only venture and look around a little. I guess you didn't want to do it alone and I can understand that. But with me now, you have no choice! You will have to adventure and explore. The challenge of the unknown excites me. Come to think of it, perhaps that explains, at least in part, my love of astronomy. In any event, I can't stand accepting things for granted. I find challenge and inquiry quite stimulating whereas people seem to prefer certainty; stick to what is familiar, known, predictable and expected. They don't want to stray out too far. Being a student of Social Work, you know that unknown and unexpected, new and novel, seem to create an unease, usher a sort of anxiety and at times may even be frightening! Anyhow, you will soon be exposed to what I mean. But to answer your question directly, Devon Square is an ethnic center where we shall arrive momentarily. Don't worry. I won't let you starve. You will have plenty of other choices if you don't like the Tandoori."

"Oh, no! I would certainly want to try. And knowing you, I can be sure that it will be a fascinating and fabulously enjoyable dinner."

14

The clear blue sky was slowly beginning to turn into myriad shades of color typical of the twilight and the breeze was getting cooler. It was a pleasant evening and people seemed to be strolling up and down, shopping, eating and looking around in a relaxed manner as Samir approached Devon Square. The car had to be parked some distance away because all vehicular traffic in Devon Square was prohibited so that people could walk freely and have a good time.

The brick pavement in the entire block was laid out in tasteful design and most shopkeepers had tables out on the pavement sprinkled with water to cool it down. The customers enjoyed sitting outside and having dinner or dessert under candlelight. The canopy light in the entire block was very soothing and the whole atmosphere instilled a feeling of festivity. People just relaxed and enjoyed this ethnic center.

There were all kinds of stores beautifully decorated in this center: authentic jewelry shops, handloom clothing and fabrics, ornaments, handicrafts, and gift items from different parts of the world. And the selection of available gourmet cuisine, fabulous desserts, and specialty confectioneries of India, Turkey, France and other lands were so enticing that the Square bustled with people sampling different delicacies and having great fun, all at reasonable prices! That was the main attraction apart from the genuine nature of the place.

Precisely as the dusk began to settle, some youngsters (looked like high school kids) appeared on the pavement of the Square offering a bouquet or a bracelet or merely a small arrangement made of freshly picked fragrant Gardenias or Jasmines to celebrate the evening. Samir bought two strings of beautifully arranged Gardenia buds, for he thought Lily's braids would look quite pretty with the *Gajras* attached to them. And Lily stood still feeling Samir's affectionate touch as he tried to fasten the Gardenia *Gajras* to her braids. She could see the romance in Samir's eyes, but said nothing. And having her braids adorned with *Gajras*, Lily looked amazingly magnetic to behold. Samir felt mighty proud as he led her up the street into Devon Square shops.

Samir was getting a little thirsty as he was introducing Lily to various shops and he asked Lily if she would like to have something cold to drink.

"Good idea. What would you suggest?"

"Have you ever tried mango *Lassi* ?"

"Never heard of it."

"Well, it's a blend of mango pulp, yogurt, some flavoring and a sweetener, a deliciously nutritious light drink. Worth a try. You might like it. But tell me first, how soon would you be ready for dinner? Now, in half an hour, or when?"

"O, in about an hour I think."

"Then, let's go have some *Lassi* and look around in some shops. OK?"

"Sounds good to me."

Samir took Lily to the stall, which catered nothing but *Lassi* freshly prepared to order while the customers watched. It seemed to be a popular cold drink, for there were many a customer standing in line and enjoying it.

"Thanks, Samir. This *Lassi* is fabulous. If I hadn't tried, I would have never known what I missed."

"I am glad you liked it. But, look! There's that International Jewelry Mart. I bet you will love to see some of the elegant jewelry designs they have. Come. Let's go in."

Even though the civilized world expected a safe and secure life, holdup, robbery and burglary were nothing unusual. Being apprehensive of such unanticipated risks, entrance into the jewelry mart was strictly regulated by electronic security system. But the shop owner knew Samir quite well because his son was a fellow student at the University (and Samir had called to let him know that Lily would be coming in to select a jewelry piece of her choice). The shop owner personally greeted Lily as she entered the shop and as a good businessman offered to show her some of the newer designs that had just arrived.

Lily was thrilled at the offer and they both sat down at the display table while the shop owner laid out dazzling diamond, ruby, emerald and sapphire sets, all so delicately crafted. Lily had never seen so many elegant precious stone sets displayed in such a manner at one sitting, marveling at the charm and beauty of great craftsmanship and design while looking at Samir in somewhat bewilderment. For she had not come here to purchase anything!

As he had preplanned, Samir readily figured out Lily's paradox and slowly whispered into her ears "Don't you like anything?" to which she quietly mumbled into Samir's ears "but I didn't come here to buy anything." "But, just for fun, let us see which one you like" Samir chuckled. "Well, I think the combination diamond-emerald set is the prettiest. What do you think?" Lily quietly asked. "You stole my heart, Lil. That's the one I liked too. It would perfectly match your emerald eyes and would be so enhancing on your fair complexion."

Samir was ecstatic as he asked the shop owner if Lily could try the emerald set to see how it looked.

"Of course, sir" the shopkeeper nodded.

And Lily first put on the diamond ring designed with tiny emerald nuggets encircling the solitaire. She then wore the matching necklace, bracelets and earrings, and with great anticipation looked into the mirror, which couldn't but reflect an overwhelmingly true expression of a typical excited bashful bride, speechless but full of emotion.

Samir was pleased seeing Lily's delightful exuberance. For this is what he wanted as a symbolic memento of his engagement with her. Having accomplished what he had set out to do, Samir signed the credit-card receipt, thanked the shop owner for being so gracious and proceeded with Lily to the Afghan Shop before heading for dinner at the

Bombay Club.

This was all so unanticipated and unimaginable for Lily that unable to reveal her emotions she just followed Samir in total silence to wherever he was taking her.

She appeared so elegant wearing the emerald-diamond set. And, Samir was so thrilled !

15

It was the Afghan Shop from where Samir had picked the casual dress Lily was wearing. But he wanted her to have something special for the dinner tonight and he very much liked the style of the attire he saw displayed at the Shop which Afghan brides wore during the engagement ceremony. So he had ordered a suit tailored in light green silk embroidered in *Zari* (golden threads) to match the size of the dress Samir had secretly borrowed from Baba.

Not letting out any secret, Samir casually mentioned to Lily as they entered the Shop that while at Devon Square he just wanted her to take a peek at this unique shop for all kinds of exceptional clothing and outfits of rich Afghan culture.

"Just look around. You may find the displays here fascinating," Samir remarked in a casual manner.

As Lily started strolling around in the Shop, the tailor

getting a hint from Samir, approached Lily and politely suggested: "Ma'am, may I have the pleasure of showing you a suit, which we just prepared for a particular customer, merely to give you an idea of embroidered designs?"

Lily looked at Samir to which he responded: "Go ahead. You might find it interesting."

And the tailor pulled out the suit from the rack and showing it to Lily, asked: "Here Ma'am. How do you like it?"

"Oh! It's so gorgeous. Never saw such an elegant embroidered dress before!"

"Just to give you a feel for it, I would request you to try it on. Would you mind?"

"No, not at all."

And the tailor directed Lily to the fitting room and gave her the suit to try.

And as Lily stepped out of the fitting room wearing the beautifully embroidered light green silk suit glittering with emerald necklace, earrings and bracelets on her delicate fair body, Samir quietly exclaimed: "Oh, my! Here comes the bride!" and even though it was not customary in Afghan culture, Samir couldn't resist kissing Lily on her forehead. Lily couldn't help turning blushed pink and feeling so shy she couldn't lift her eyes to meet Samir's tender expressions. But she soon recovered and looking directly at Samir she smiled and said in a soft voice: "Samir, I thought you were so simple. But you have proven to be incorrigible and a bit devious at that! I don't know whether I can handle you, Samir!"

"Never mind, Lily! You don't have to handle me. Suffice, if I can handle you! That should be good enough, don't you think?"

"And you are so haughty and naughty all at the same time. I don't know what I can do with you!"

"Right now, you can't do anything with me. But I do not underrate your prowess when it will be your turn! However, we will settle this later. Let's go for dinner now. It's getting late."

And looking like an anxious Afghan bride, all dressed up and overwhelmed, Lily proceeded with Samir in complete silence to the Bombay Club.

Samir was quietly happy that his plans were working perfect.

16

The Bombay Club specialized in Tandoori delicacies. It was a very popular restaurant. The decor and the atmosphere were elegantly pleasant and they had live music over the weekend. When Lily and Samir arrived, the *sitar* and violin were just being tuned and the ensemble was getting ready for the performance. Samir had reserved a choice table close to the dais in the music hall where dinner was served so that Lily could catch every note of the *Ragas* being played, for that was the essence of the melody. The harmonious accompaniment of *Tabla* accentuated the rhythm that *Ragas* created. It was a performance of excellence for which the Bombay Club was particularly acclaimed.

After presenting some classical selections, the group also played popular tunes to which the patrons could dance and have fun.

Being a total stranger to Tandoori cuisine, Lily had to rely on Samir to decide whatever he thought she would relish (after all, it was entirely Samir's agenda and it was all so unexpected. So, this might as well be his choice, Lily reasoned to herself).

"Have you picked from the menu what you would like to have?"

"No, I don't know what to select. Allow me to depend on you, Samir. Please go ahead and order for me."

"You might regret my taste. It's a bit on the adventurous side as you may have gathered by now."

"Don't worry. I have full faith and patience; faith in your tasteful choice and patience for your adventurous side! Besides, even after reading the menu, I am unable to decide what would be a good selection. So go ahead. The hostess seems to be waiting for your order."

And Samir ordered *Samosas* as appetizers, Tandoori shrimp, chicken *tikka*, *sag-paneer* (a spinach preparation), *bharta* (an eggplant preparation), *dal-makhni* (a legume preparation), Basmati rice and *Nan*.

And while they were enjoying the appetizer, the music started and as the ensemble got into full swing playing *Raga Kirvani, Kaharva Taal*, Lily couldn't help getting totally immersed in it, listening with rapt attention to the melody of notes magically reverberating from the *sitar* as if the *Raga* was echoing deep within her. And, touching Samir at his arm, she whispered: "Samir, I cannot tell you exactly, but this *Raga* has such quality that it seems to infiltrate and touch the very soul. I feel an ecstatic sense of exaltation, of delightful rapture. It seems to lift you in a state of being totally removed from the mundane. Do you feel the same way?"

"Precisely. That's why I brought you here. For I felt you had the sensitivity to absorb the affect of *Ragas*."

Just then the hostess arrived with dinner prepared to order and served hot.

Lily was delighted to have such a sumptuous dinner. It was all a novelty for her but she thoroughly enjoyed the delicious preparations. It was then that the hostess requested Lily to follow her to the fabulously enticing dessert table arranged next to the dance floor at the center of the music hall. Samir had requested a special cake for the occasion and as Lily approached the dessert table, the hostess opening the Champagne bottle announced to the assembly to give a big hand to the newly engaged couple as Lily cut the cake. The ensemble struck a swinging tune and Samir snatched Lily on to the dance floor under thunderous applause and clapping of the amused assembly.

Lily sparkled in her emerald-green Afghan attire as she gracefully danced under the radiant chandeliers. Samir was exquisitely charming as he paced with ease on the dance floor holding Lily romantically.

17

The night was beautiful as Samir was driving back from Devon Square toward home. The silvery moon was bright in the clear sky and the mild breeze was invigorating.

"I don't know Samir, but I still can't reconcile to the unusual events of the day. It was so unimaginable and unexpected that it all seems so unreal," said Lily as she moved next to Samir in the car.

"Love without expression remains hidden. And, secret, unanticipated revelations are sweeter, Lily" Samir proffered a rationale for what had occurred during the day.

"I understand now why you were so evasive to my questions. But even more thrilling is the discovery of the hidden soft side of my Samir! And, now by your own admission, I can certainly expect and demand greater expression of your love. Correct?"

"You certainly may demand, but compliance is another matter, Ma'am."

"Well, sir, if you don't, I won't."

"Looks like you are preparing grounds for a battle, maybe for a war!"

"No, only for a strategy to winning one!"

And while such sweet talk continued, Samir suddenly turned the car into the entrance to the "Camp Grounds" and said to Lily: "Here we are. Ready for the battle?"

"But, Samir, I didn't prepare for camping at all."

"You didn't need to. I did. There is a tent, sleeping bag, water bottle, blankets and a pair of pajamas in the trunk. And above all, there is the bright moon inviting us for sweet slumber under the peaceful spread of this perfect night in these meadows, you will agree," and "remember, you said 'why don't people come out of their apartment life and camp out amidst the wonderful bounty of nature's gift?' and so here we are."

"Ah! The night is really beautiful in these meadows and the touch of cool, calm breeze totally unwinds me," said Lily as she looked into the depth of the meadows.

"And how did you think of camping out here tonight?" asked an anxious Lily.

"Shouldn't I have? Don't you wish that I should have? In any event, I always carry the camping gear in the trunk and sometimes when it gets late while returning from the Observatory and the weather is perfect with the moonlit sky, I just camp out in these meadows looking at the stars. It just relaxes me and stimulates my mind to creative thinking. And now, you being with me under the charm of these meadows, I thought it would be a heavenly experience. Come, let's set up the tent."

And taking care not to spoil her Afghan dress, Lily helped Samir to put up the tent on a clear secluded patch of the meadow. Thereafter, Lily went into the tent and changed into the pajamas Samir had brought. As she was putting on the pajamas, Lily felt nervous imagining what the night in the camp was likely to be! And, aroused with some fantasy about Samir, she carefully took off the jewelry, folded the Afghan dress and set them all aside in a corner. In the mean time Samir unfolded the sleeping bag, stretched the blankets, changed into shorts and got ready to retire.

This was the first time they were together in the isolation of a quiet night and as they looked at each other, an irresistible sensation seemed to instantly pervade both of them and Samir gently pulled Lily closer within the fold of his arms.

Lily was all excited and Samir's mere touch stirred a

sensory shiver all over her body and looking into Samir's eyes she softly spoke: "This was the moment I have been waiting for, Samir. I longed for your touch, for your feel, for your embrace all day but I was helpless! Oh! you don't know how much I miss not having you, Samir!" and so murmuring Lily gently touched Samir's lips with her own, folding her arms round him which inevitably thrust Lily's throbbing breasts against Samir's wide-open chest. Feeling the warmth of Lily's engorged body and the wetness of her warm lips, Samir pulled Lily even closer and held her tight with affectionate embrace gliding his fingers through her soft silken hair. Samir's every touch was arousing an anxious convulsion throughout her body and Lily was beginning to get nervous with an unknown desire silently compelling her to be responsive to the sensual pressure of Samir's strong but tender muscular body as she began to breathe heavy.

"Touch me, feel me all over. Let my womanhood blossom into its ultimate purpose. Let our bodies merge so that the union of our soul be complete," Lily was murmuring in soft whispering sounds as Samir began to gently explore and caress Lily. Every touch of his warm lips and tender fingers stirred a deep quivering sensation, which made Lily pull Samir even closer until she longingly felt Samir's irresistible smooth thrust into her body, which culminated in giving both of them an orgasmic excitation of immense ecstatic pleasure relaxing their tense anticipation.

The moon was still visible through the tent screen and neither of them knew when or how they fell asleep in the silence of the night cuddled together.

18

The birds began singing with the break of the dawn and Samir and Lily woke up getting ready to head back to the University.

"Perhaps it is inexplicable Lily, but I can't help feeling that our shared single body last night was a natural climactic perfection of our love. And from a social perspective my only wish now is to consolidate it in customary matrimonial bond. That's all I desire and that's all I want."

"So do I, Samir. Maybe it is all mysterious, but Samir, don't you think it is the union of the bodies that culminates into the union of soul? Isn't it the intense, exciting moment of warm affection and physical fulfillment that impels a feeling of inseparable attachment and ushers a sense of eternal belonging? I don't know Samir how it all relates but for me it was a consummating, ecstatic night of immense meaning and significance for which I long forever! For me love is the language, luster and liaison of life, Samir."

"I do not know whether it is conceivable but I can't imagine life without you, Lily. You are the personification of my love and embodiment of my dreams, Lil," and so saying Samir gently kissed Lily and continued: "now, planning our wedding is my first priority. But, while I plan for the wedding and honeymoon, I have got to organize and announce this month's Sunday Forum."

"I think Professor Henry Watson has finally agreed to address the Forum," Samir continued. "He was quite reluctant to accept the invitation, for he did not wish to stir the controversy any more than necessary. However, the global importance and seminal public policy aspects of the issues persuaded him to discuss the subject matter in its true perspective. He suggested the title of his presentation be: "Should Human Genetic Engineering be Banned?" He was concerned that some fundamentalist religious group may create trouble but that was all the more reason, Dr. Watson thought, to have an open factual discussion so as to allay the wide-spread misconception and misunderstanding of this futuristic science and technology. I think, Lily, it will be of immense interest to the public to have the author of this frontier research address the scientific, moral, ethical and legal issues so much sensationalized by the media, the politicians, the clergies and the critics."

"It is absolutely a subject of topical importance and we are fortunate to have Dr. Watson agree to address the Forum and set the record straight. So the Forum must now make careful preparations for his presentation," Lily readily concurred with Samir.

"And for the honeymoon, I want to be at the *Taj Mahal* and then on the houseboat in Kashmir," Lily added quickly to keep Samir on track.

"I shall comply," Samir smiled reassuringly, adding: "but the choice of your clothing will be mine."

"I would love to be adorned and adored in any manner you desire. It would be a pleasure satisfying your dreams, sir!" Lily retorted smilingly.

"I know why you want to be so mellow, for you know I would be imaginative."

"Absolutely. But regardless, I shall be the winner," Lily asserted.

And talking over such things, they arrived at Lily's house.

Lily quickly put some hot water for tea and requested Baba to warm up some bagel for Samir while Lily took out some cream cheese and jelly from the refrigerator. Lily preferred cracked wheat toast with tea.

The morning was still young and soon after finishing breakfast Samir wanted to go to the University to check out his mailbox in the Department prior to heading to his room.

"Don't worry. I shall take care of the announcement for Dr. Watson's Forum lecture and arrange everything," said Samir as he got into the car.

"So long. I shall see you soon," Lily waved goodbye to Samir as the car started.

19

The lecture hall was packed with audience for Dr. Watson's lecture. Indeed, people were standing anywhere they could find a place, all seats having been taken by those arriving early. In order to avoid any commotion or unrest, it was imperative that the program started on time. Hence, exactly at 7:30 p.m., Lily entered the stage with Dr. Watson amid thunderous applause greeting them.

"Thank you, thank you very much, ladies and gentlemen for your warm welcome to Dr. Watson," began Lily standing at the microphone. And introducing Dr. Watson she continued: "We are honored to have Professor Henry Watson with us this evening to present his thoughts on genomics and bioengineering with particular reference to its human application. As you know Dr. Watson is on the forefront of this technology and he is a world-renowned authority on the subject. Lately, the government, the media critics and religious leaders have raised some issues with human genetic engineering on moral, ethical and legal grounds and there exists some controversy on the subject. What better than to have the authority on the subject address the issues and clarify the controversy? So ladies and gentlemen, I am proud to present to you Professor Henry Watson, Director of the Laboratory for Genetic Engineering at the University. The topic of his presentation is: 'Should Human Genetic Engineering be Banned?' Please give him a warm welcome."

And the audience greeted Dr. Watson with a standing ovation as he came forward to the microphone. Dr. Watson then began: "Thank you very much, ladies and gentlemen! I am humbled at the overwhelming warmth bestowed upon me and I thank Lily for inviting me to address this distinguished gathering."

"Let me now attempt to get directly into the heart of the subject. I shall try to define the issues, present the facts, and then analyze the controversies in light of the facts."

"So, what are the issues? What is it that bothers the people? What is so objectionable about human genetic engineering that it should be banned and public support be denied for its study and research?"

"In simple terms, genetic engineering is nothing more than manipulation of the genes. And this manipulation can take any of several forms from altering the genes, to regulating, transferring or replacing genetic material by physical, chemical or biological means, or by controlling genetic expression with whatever methods that may be appropriate and desirable."

"And the genes are nothing more than an assemblage of a particular chemical called DNA. It is this DNA, which is the chemical basis of life. You can take a complete set of this genetic material, that is a complete assemblage of DNA, what we call as 'genome', put it in a competent cell, for example an enucleated egg, or other vehicle as may be necessary, and create a new life. This manipulation is also known as 'nuclear transfer'. An aspect of such manipulation is called "Cloning," which is a method of asexual reproduction, taking a pre-existing complete set of genetic material, the genome, from a non-reproductive somatic cell and making this genetic material become regenerative, thereby producing a genetically identical copy of the donor wherefrom the complete set of genetic material was obtained. Successful cloning has been accomplished in plants and in such vertebrates as lambs, mice, pigs, goats, cows, monkeys, rabbits and a pet cat."

"It may be important to note here for argument's sake that even if cloning of humans were possible and perfected, cloning will only produce look-alike persons, *but not identical personalities*, for the simple reason that behavior patterns and personality traits are also dependent among other factors on socio-environmental surroundings, which are ever changing and never alike from one moment to the other. Of course, the final formation or complete development of an organism is an outcome of the interaction between the genes and the developmental environment. Thus, even the most perfect clones produced by 'Nature' in the form of monozygotic twins, are never found to possess identical behavior patterns, temperament or personalities because as I just mentioned, the developmental conditions to which the zygotes and the socio-environmental surroundings to which the born individuals are exposed, are never exactly alike. Hence, it is a great big fallacy that cloning will produce an army of "Hitlerian Robots." It is a theoretical as well as a practical impossibility. Those who raise such specter are simply uninformed of the science and the workings of the methodology."

"I readily concede that it is hard to realize and difficult to accept that what we call life is nothing more than an interactive expression of the genome, the complete set of genetic material made of DNA. Successful cloning of higher forms of animals and even more remarkably, producing in the laboratory a live virus possessing all the attributes of its naturally occurring counterpart, simply from a written blueprint of DNA letters, abundantly demonstrates that no supernatural, divine or providential participation is necessary to create life, unless you take the extreme and rather untenable position of ascribing providential attributes to this inanimate chemical called DNA. And just so that you know, this DNA is nothing more than a composition of three rather simple chemical entities: a sugar, a phosphate and a nitrogen base, formed in a particular sequential order and structure. I am not at all surprised at the fact that for anyone not exposed to or enunciated in the science of molecular biology, recognition of the *physical* basis of life is "UnGodly." But allow me to point out that the songs of the birds, the roar of the lion and the secretions of hormones setting in motion the intense emotional activity to cuddle and mate are all inherent expressions of the genome through its self-regulatory processes of growth and development. And all that happens as a result of sexual reproduction is a random assortment and combination of genes thereby giving rise to diverse genotypes expressed in diverse phenotypes. Hence, no two organisms are ever found identical unless monozygotic or asexually reproduced. It is a fundamental fact that we, as all organisms, are in the final analysis expressions of individual genomes in a given environment. And it is the decoding of the human genome and determining the function of genes embodied therein that shall reveal the secrets of our "Being," as it has already done to a certain extent. And it will be through the study of this genetic material that we shall learn the biological bases of human species. It is this knowledge which will tell us what governs our destiny, longevity, bodily features, disease processes, intelligence and the like. And, only through the tools of genetic engineering shall we be able to accomplish gene replacement, correct genetic errors, cure diseases, alter or improve the genetic makeup as appropriate, necessary or desirable. Endowed with such most fundamental knowledge constituting the very essence of human existence, can it stand to reason that we refuse, discard, deny or wish away the reality, promise and potential of biotechnology?"

"What we have learned, therefore, is that to unravel the mysteries of life processes and to create life, what is required is the study of the genomic material. And with the completion of the "Human Genome Project," the entire DNA sequence of human genes is available for whatever purpose it is to be used. And this is what leads to the controversy."

"It is asserted by some that human genetic engineering may be unethical, immoral and illegal, that it flouts "Human Dignity" and that "Man is Playing God." Such issues have arisen pointedly with respect to "Human Cloning."

"Let me respectfully ask, why is it immoral or unethical to produce an identical copy of an individual through "cloning," if it is not immoral, illegal or unethical to produce a baby through artificial insemination, in vitro fertilization, frozen human embryos and through genetically manipulated custom made embryos from unfamiliar sperm and egg donors at fertility clinics and to have a surrogate mother bear a child? And it is still more intriguing that society does not find it immoral, illegal or unethical to give birth to a fetus *determined and destined* to have serious birth defects, debilitating deformities and life-threatening *terminal* genetic anomaly, but considers producing a *normal* healthy cloned individual to be immoral, illegal and unethical!"

"Human cloning may never become a household reality. Nevertheless, perfection of reliable, safe techniques would offer not only an alternative reproductive modality to humans but also allow unique possibilities and advantages not otherwise feasible or available. For instance, successful cloning and haploidization will usher in an era of immortality and resurrection of life, perhaps not even conceptualized by opponents! And, how could the safety and reliability, two foremost issues of great concern to society, ever be determined unless human trial is attempted after careful research?"

"Some argue, though, that even if a normal baby is born through cloning, down the road it may be prone to serious deformities or ailments if cloned animal experiments are any guide. This seems to be an unwarranted specter because there is no certainty that despite all available genetic and prenatal tests, a normal-looking baby born of *natural birth* won't develop a debilitating condition down the road and succumb to premature death. All that can be done in cloned pregnancy, therefore, is to take all possible screening and precautionary measures with ultrasound, amniocentesis and other techniques for fetal monitoring as are used in natural pregnancy. Thus, there can be no greater risk in a cloned pregnancy than in a natural one in as much as the prenatal diagnostic tests known to medical science are indicative and prognostic of fetal health."

"Furthermore, it may be well to recognize in this context that even 'Mother Nature' doesn't always produce perfectly normal babies. Indeed, genetic aspects of cancer, aging, heart disease, mental disorders and many other human ailments, suffering and infirmities reveal that to the extent predisposition, probabilities or susceptibilities are involved, these are inevitable and unpredictable consequences resulting from the hereditary mechanisms of independent assortment and random combination of genes inherent in the modality of the normal sexual reproductive process. Clearly, everything that 'Nature' does, including mutations, is not always desirable, beneficial or preferable. But for these reasons and unavoidable genetic risks, should the procreative phase, distinct from the intense pleasurable aspect of natural human egg-sperm union, be forbidden in favor of other safer, predictable and tested reproductive technologies?"

"Perhaps it is the negation of commonly held notions and beliefs, the fear of the new and novel rather than of rational reasoning that produces irreconcilable dichotomies in socio-legal thought. And aren't such dichotomies the result of misunderstanding, misconception and sheer ignorance of the basics of science and technology? It certainly does not seem to emanate from an abiding reverence to "Nature" because man has been playing God from time immemorial, ever since he began to master the forces of Nature. Imagine what would be the human destiny if man stopped playing God and a victim of heart attack was never resuscitated, or heart, liver or kidney transplants were forbidden, or artificial lung, heart and kidney machines were not utilized during serious surgical procedures to save and prolong life. Indeed, conquest over Nature's inflictions and playing God may be the ultimate virtue of human efforts and ingenuity!"

"And God, even if there is one, must remain pre-occupied with the bigger task of managing and controlling His continuously inflating and exploding vast Universe-Multiverse, leaving the happenings on the tiny remote planet Earth to its autonomous processes, maintaining the magnanimity of remaining above the local fray of trivial 'Earthly' matters! For having the awesome responsibility of monitoring and regulating the ferociously fiery upheavals constantly going on in His unimaginably vast cosmos, God just couldn't afford the luxury of sparing time to be bothered with puerile idiosyncrasies of human species; leaving them rather free and at liberty to jolly well do whatever they felt like doing! And it appears humans have unhesitatingly taken full advantage of their God's liberal latitude!

"Although there isn't much that can be argued about one's belief and faith, which are usually immutable, and it may be disagreeable to most folks, nevertheless, to put it differently in terms of a mathematical phrase, perpetuation of God's domain seems inversely related to the depth, sophistication and knowledge of natural and biophysical sciences, and the strength of analytical mind possessed by humans. Indeed, men created God precisely because they did not understand natural forces and phenomena and they needed something to cope with fearsome anxiety and nature's inimical tempestuous displays. Imaginary conceptualization of God provided a secure feeling and fulfilled the instinctive need of human mind for comfort, consolation and courage in the face of adversity. Faith, worship and prayer evolved as an assuring and tranquilizing mechanism to ward off anxiety and tide over distress, fear and fatality. Hence, to that extent the unreal became a reality."

"The fact is that human effort, endeavor and decisions are often based more on self-preservation and satisfying fulfillment of economic and materialistic needs, rather than on scriptural-religious underpinnings. And is it not an absurdity of moral, religious, ethical and legal high ground that society allows scores of healthy robust individuals in the prime of their lives to get addicted to smoke-emitting nicotine products and to die premature cancerous deaths but doesn't dare banning it while objecting to individual choice of having a cloned baby? Even with the inevitable certainty of unquestionable risk associated with deadly addiction, if we are free to make individual choices in one arena, aren't we free to make choices in another arena of enormous relevance to the very essence of humanity?"

"In summary, it is the knowledge of human genetic code and the ability to manipulate, regulate, control or influence the genetic expression that will equip man to be the master of his own destiny. Granted that there would have to be safeguards against abuse and misuse, but society should be mature and responsible enough to let human reason, imagination, intellect and ingenuity reach its ultimate full potential. For it could never be held bondage forever to suffocation or repression by societal decree. Human spirit is simply indomitable and humans will ultimately achieve what is achievable. It is only a truism that what could be done, will be done. I call this innate human urge as the '*Law of Eventual Accomplishment*'."

"It is quite likely that this will be interpreted by some as an atheist scheme. Notwithstanding such antagonism, may I respectfully submit, ladies and gentlemen, that I have proffered this elaborate exposition not to promote any particular position, but only because there seems to exist so much lack of knowledge and improper understanding of science and its principles. Indeed, there appears to be a concerted effort to feed dis- and mis-information to the people for emotional appeal based often on personal beliefs rather than on facts, simply to seek public support for other than scientific reasons. It almost seems as though we are not prepared to face or accept the objectivity and fundamental discoveries of scientific inquiry! I am optimistic, however, that reason will prevail over prejudice."

"Thank you, ladies and gentlemen, for listening to me," and concluding his remarks Dr. Watson began retreating from the microphone toward his seat when a stream of gunshots appeared to strike him from behind and he collapsed on the stage! Lily jumped immediately trying to shield Dr. Watson who was still conscious, but bleeding from his intestinal cavity. Samir rushed through the pandemonium ensuing in the lecture hall from the gunshots, joining Lily and calling an ambulance for immediate transfer of Dr. Watson to the Emergency Room. People were panicked and frantically rushing out of the lecture hall to safety while all attention of University personnel was being focused on protecting Dr. Watson and clearing the path for the ambulance to pick up Dr. Watson and rush him to the hospital. It was all very chaotic.

The news of Dr. Watson having been shot spread like wild fire throughout the city. The perpetrators seemed to have escaped cleverly. No suspects were immediately identified nor any arrests made, although police and detectives were engaged in an intense investigation.

The entire community was stunned with shock and surprise.

20

Two bullets were found lodged in Dr. Watson's body, miraculously sparing his vital organs. After surgery Dr. Watson was listed in critical but stable condition. Prognosis for his recovery was good and everyone was relieved that Dr. Watson would survive the murderous gunshots.

As usual the radio, television and newspapers were all outraged expressing anger and frustration at the culture of violence permeating the social fabric. But nobody proposed or advocated banning the sale of firearms and assault weapons, the means for committing crime and violence.

Lily was shaken to the core from witnessing the shocking episode and realizing how fragile life could be at the hands of some zealot or fanatic who could abruptly reduce life to nullity, as the shooting of Dr. Watson flashed through her mind's eye.

"It's an unacceptable social condition, Samir, that despite regulatory laws anyone could obtain a gun and shoot anybody they got mad at or didn't like or agree with, or whose ideas were unconventional, challenging or revolutionary," expressed a perturbed Lily asking Samir whether the police had any leads or clues.

"The police suspect the involvement of a fundamentalist religious group called "The God's Children" who are known to be vocal and opposed to Professor Watson's work. The detectives surmise that the group believed Professor Watson to be an accomplished researcher and a brilliant scientist of great achievements who could accomplish what he postulated, and finding his presentation at the Sunday Forum as going a little bit too far against God, it might have triggered them to "wipe him out," Samir explained the theory police were working on. "Of course, the group is well knit and zealously protective of their members. Hence, it is not going to be easy to identify the perpetrators, for they must have carefully planned their exit after firing the shots," Samir added.

"Regardless of the theories, the basic problem is the availability of these deadly means of killing people. And it is high time that we stopped it."

"And how do you propose to accomplish that?"

"I have thought through it and I know how," responded a confident Lily. "But you have to help me call a general meeting of the student body," Lily continued, adding: "I know the students are all upset that this could happen at the University and to a person like Dr. Watson, whom they cherish with utmost regard as a professor and scientist of great vision, intellect, honesty and integrity."

"And what will be the agenda for the general meeting, Lily?"

"Close the gun shops!" Lily was emphatic.

"Do you realize that this is not as simple and achievable as you might think? Besides, you are asking to take on a well financed, politically connected and highly organized membership."

"I am not underestimating anything. But do you know that the more powerful an adversary (I do not wish to call them "enemy"), the more successful our struggle will be? And all I ask is that you be with me through thick and thin."

"You hurt me immensely and break my heart Lily, when you say such a thing. How could you ever imagine that I shall not be with you? Never again speak such words, my Lil" and so saying Samir gently embraced Lily and kissed her softly.

21

Dr. Watson's wounds were healing rapidly and he was progressing well after surgery, beginning to receive friends, colleagues and well-wishers who wanted to visit him at the hospital. He was especially moved by the out-pouring of "Get Well" cards, letters and messages from all over the world, particularly from his esteemed colleagues with whom he collaborated in research and study. Dr. Watson developed a deep sense of love and respect for Lily and Samir's devoted efforts to save his life by rushing him to the emergency room and following up with every detail until the return of Dr. Watson to the recovery room after surgery and visiting him every morning and evening thereafter to make sure that all was going well. Dr. Watson was so humble and modest in his ways that he didn't know exactly how to express his gratitude to these two young individuals, except that he would look at them and hold their hands with a loving smile whenever they would come to visit him.

On the day Dr. Watson was scheduled to be discharged from the hospital, Lily and Samir let it be known to him their detailed plans and strategies to stop the sale of murderous weapons. Stirred by the purpose of their cause requiring resolute determination and extreme sacrifice, Dr. Watson simply said : "I commend your courageous dedication Lily and ask you only one favor: Would you allow me to be recruited as one of your abiding lieutenants? I shall try my utmost not to let you down," and with those sentiments Dr. Watson got up from the wheel chair and left for his home in the car waiting for him outside the patient lobby.

Lily's eyes were wet as she waved goodbye to Dr. Watson.

"I just can't get over it, Samir. His words are echoing in my mind. I can't believe that Dr. Watson himself wants to be a part of the campaign," said Lily turning to Samir as Dr. Watson's car pulled out.

"He is a man of great conscience and having seen death so closely, a different sense of purpose must have stirred him deep inside," Samir explained.

"I am elated, Samir, because his participation will make it a formidable campaign. I know now exactly how to proceed. Calling the general meeting of the student body is now the top priority."

"I have already made an announcement and circulars are being posted everywhere throughout the campus. I expect a huge gathering. From whatever little feedback I am getting, they all seem excited about the agenda. They think it will be "cool" to take on the 'Monster'!"

"I am just psyched, Samir."

"I know how excited you are. But I am feeling a bit hungry. Let's go to the cafeteria and pick up something quick to eat. We have a lot of planning and organizing to do."

And they both proceeded toward the Student Union cafeteria to grab a quick bite.

Samir and Lily were familiar faces to almost everyone in the cafeteria and acknowledging greetings of everyone with a "Hi", "Hello", or with the wave of a hand, they picked up some soup and salad and headed out toward Lily's office in the Administration Building.

Hot soup with whole-wheat crackers was Samir's favorite and as he stirred the soup with the spoon, he said to Lily: "The student body meeting has been called for this coming Saturday at 2 p.m. in the sports complex. Some group leaders have indicated a desire to present their views and requested time to address the gathering. I think this is indicative of great interest and enthusiasm on the part of the student body."

"Absolutely. Let everyone who wishes to speak come forward and express their feelings. The more the participation, the more cohesive, deeper and solid our strength will be," Lily agreed munching on salad.

"We must plan now how the meeting shall be conducted. Let's put our heads together and chalk out a plan of action, OK?" Samir suggested.

"But first I would like to have a good hot cup of tea. I am going to the Office kitchenette to fix a cup for me. Would you care to have some? I will fix it the way you like it. What do you say?" Lily looked at Samir with a tease on her face.

"I dare not refuse a good offer coming from a lovely lady," Samir smiled, and while having tea they discussed their plans for the upcoming gathering of the student body.

22

The sports complex had a big open field for such games as football, soccer and baseball. And on this Saturday it was getting full with the students. By 2 p.m. the stadium was packed. The eagerness and enthusiasm of the students were unmistakable.

Precisely at 2 p.m., in his capacity as the President of the student body, Samir brought the meeting to order. Then, addressing the vast gathering as he looked from one side of the stadium to the other, Samir began: "Dear friends and colleagues! Please allow me, first, to express my sincere gratitude to all of you for responding in short notice to my call for this meeting. Besides that, however, there is one person, I dare say, who can be squarely held responsible for this unprecedented state of affairs! He was targeted to be dead but somehow he has survived the assassin's bullets! And you know who that is. It is this frail-looking gentleman sitting by my side, Professor Henry Watson," and pointing to Dr. Watson, Samir requested: "Professor Watson, would you kindly come to the microphone and acknowledge your presence?"

Professor Watson stood up and as he waved at the students, a thunderous applause of "Long Live Watson, Long Live Watson" filled the stadium.

Dr. Watson was visibly moved by such outpouring of affection and addressing the students he said in a subdued voice: "My dear students, I am deeply touched and humbled by the love you have showered on me and at the moment I am simply incapable of holding back my emotions and adequately expressing my feelings. But let Samir conduct the meeting and I shall speak to you just in a little while," and so saying Dr. Watson sat down and Samir took over the microphone.

"At this point let me present to you Meira Rosen, a senior at the School of Law who will lay out the premise, purpose, goals and objectives of our gathering this afternoon."

"Meira, please come forward," and with those remarks Samir took his seat.

"My fellow students! I am not here to present an elaborate argument or a complicated thesis on what is so self-evident: that guns, pistols, rifles and firearms of all sorts are meant for one purpose, and one purpose only, that is to kill people. Since we live in an imperfect world where military power and armies do exist and where 'might is right' still prevails as *modus operandi*, whether we like it or not, the use of force appears to be a reality no matter how it is justified or rationalized; whether for self-defense, national or economic interest, for peace keeping, to curb territorial expansion, aggression or terror. Therefore, one can see why soldiers and armies have to be equipped with these weapons. But is there any reason why, in a civil society, such murderous weapons are made available to ordinary citizens? It certainly cannot be for peoples' protection, otherwise why would we need the police force? Indeed, isn't it true that the more the guns are allowed in open circulation, the lesser the self-protection and the more of murders, maiming and killings?" Meira asked challenging the self-protection premise for selling the guns.

"Some argue that it is not the guns that kill people, rather it is the people who kill people! I call this a patently bogus semantics. Tell me, if it were not for the guns and pistols, how else Mahatma Gandhi, John Kennedy, Martin Luther King, Anwar Sadat, Yitzak Rabin and many others would have been killed?" Meira asked amid loud cheers.

"I say, stop trumpery and face the facts," Meira responded emphatically to the cheers.

"And some argue that guns are sold because it is a necessity for hunting. First, killing animals for fun is a cruel sport. Nevertheless, if hunting has to be done, let the government rent the guns to registered licensed hunters during the hunting season for specific hours from designated gun-posts near the hunting grounds and when the hunting is over, the rented guns are returned to the gun-posts. Isn't that a simple solution? So then, where is the necessity for anyone to own and possess a gun? Therefore, I say again, stop the excuses and admit the false pretenses. How long are you going to hide behind the fictitious facade of frivolous arguments, I ask the gun lobbyists?" Meira retorted.

"We hear every day how innocent people are shot dead, how ordinary folks are threatened, abused and terrorized at the gun-point. Indeed, we don't have to go very far. Look right here. We had just about lost to the bullets a world-renowned scientist of extraordinary talent and achievements, our own Professor Watson. Tell me, how long are we going to tolerate this gun-culture? My fellow students, enough is enough! There is no place for guns in a civil society and we are going to stop it right here!" And, so saying Meira took her seat while the students kept applauding with spirited ovation.

Samir then introduced John Hamilton, a graduate student in the School of Economics to express his views.

"You know, my fellow students, it's all about money! This gun-establishment, these weapons traders, they don't care about human life, they don't care about morals, they don't care about ethics. They don't care about anything. All they care about is profiteering. There is so much money involved in manufacturing and selling these unabashed means of violence, that they wish to protect and perpetuate this moneymaking machine, this very lucrative industry. And they have figured out exactly how to accomplish this. You know what they do? Being fully aware that a politician's survival depends on campaign financing, they contribute large sums of money to the politicians' election chest, directly or indirectly. And we sure do know that money buys everything. Politicians are no exception. By donating huge sums, they obligate the politicians to protect their interest. Money talks, and talks big, doesn't it?" John retorted.

"It's a shame on our modernity that as our civilization progresses, we harbor more, not less, means of violence! Isn't the culture of violence a global and human tragedy? Must we endorse the trade, the business, the occupation and the pastime of violence? Must we tolerate a social structure where the fear of loose cannons pervades our daily lives? And, do you think the government, the rulers and these professional politicians care for you and me? Let me tell you something. They are interested first and foremost in one thing and one thing only, that is to preserve, perpetuate and protect their own position and power."

"So here is what we do," John continued. "In this coming election, which is just around the corner, we nominate our own representative to the parliament and with our voting strength of greater than 30,000, we will throw out the rascals, the incumbents," John declared and the students applauded with elation, chanting: "we want Lily, we want Lily!"

Samir tried to calm down the gathering but the chanting continued until Lily came forward and acknowledged with a loud voice raising her hand: "I accept your nomination. Thank you, thank you very much for your trust and confidence in me."

Just then, as Lily was speaking, Professor Watson suddenly got up grabbing Lily's raised hand and summoning all his energies, thundered through the microphone: "I second your nomination," and the students arose *en masse* in a triumphant jubilation. The whole stadium seemed to burst with joy and excitement.

And when the quiet returned, Professor Watson continued: "I shall not take much of your time but I would like to make a confession before you," and with a brief pause Dr. Watson looked at the gathering and said: "I have seen death so closely that it has emancipated me. They can come and kill me now, but they are not going to keep me from reiterating the fundamental fact that everything that is required to make and mould a human being is written in our DNA and it is the mathematically rigorous *methods* of science, not the edicts of scriptures, that shall lead us to discover the ultimate reality, the true nature of things," and with those remarks Dr. Watson took his seat.

It was a sobering experience for the students as they heard Dr. Watson's succinct words in rapt attention. Thereafter, Samir thanked the gathering and the meeting was adjourned.

23

Lily and Samir were still trying to catch their breath as they came out of the meeting. They couldn't believe how potent Meira, John and Dr. Watson's words were and how so concisely they articulated the issues. And it was still more surprising how spontaneous, enthusiastic and cohesive the gathering's response was.

"I really did not expect the way things turned out," Samir admitted at the outcome of the meeting. "What an event it was when the stadium echoed with the chorus: 'we want Lily, we want Lily'", a thrilled Samir recollected as he pulled Lily closer with a mischievous smile: "I didn't know you were that popular! You sure have some influence, don't you?"

"Get alerted, Samir. My influence is more pervasive than you realize!" Lily retorted with equal mischief in her inviting eyes. "The challenge now is to harness this huge political power in a constructive manner," Lily was pensive as she continued: "a united voting strength of more or less 30,000 counts can shake up the establishment. And make no mistake, the vested interests will find every means possible to incite and break apart this unity," Lily added in a serious note.

"I know it quite well, Lil. When it comes to threatening their very existence and survival, no laws, no morals, no ethics, no dignity, no values, nothing will matter. They will use every trick, fair or foul, to discredit and disrupt our campaign. That's the nature of the beast, of dirty politics, as some call it, Lily. But that doesn't bother me. All we have to do is to be ever more open and vigilant. The more transparent and open our approach, the greater the adversary's problems and the lesser our worries," Samir was thoughtful.

"I couldn't agree more, Samir. Give the Devil a rope and it will hang itself! That's the formula that is going to work perfect. If they play dirty, they will incur peoples' wrath and bury themselves. If they play civil, we shall prevail. Either way, it's a win-win situation for us," Lily surmised.

“The electorate is pretty smart. They will figure out what’s going on,” Samir concurred.

“But you know Lil, you are going to be twenty eight next week. Trying to catch up with me, Yeh? I am always twenty-nine, mine never changes! How about celebrating it before we get deeply involved in our campaign? This time there will be no surprises. The birthday party shall be at your house, OK?” Samir suggested.

“You sure, you want to do that?”

“Absolutely! How can I not do it?”

“But then, I expect Mummy and Papa to be there too.”

“That’s even better. Let them celebrate your birthday and I shall join in the fun and enjoyment. But let me know if, for some reason, they were not going to make it so that I can arrange things with Baba’s help. All right?”

“OK.”

The evening was drawing closer and Samir wanted to unwind from the consuming schedule of the day. So he said to Lily: “Let’s go to a nice restaurant and have a good meal. It’s time to relax a little. Do you have any preference, Ma’am?” Samir asked with a grin.

“In fact, I do, sir! Would you believe, I am in a mood to have Thai food tonight!”

“That’s an excellent choice. I know that `Bangkok Delight’ is not too far and they have a great menu. So Thai food it shall be. Let’s go.”

The weather was perfect with a light breeze blowing under the clear sky turning pinkish-orange near the western horizon where the sun was about to set. The birds were beginning to settle on the trees lining the street, which was not too crowded. Although there was the subway from the University to Victoria Crossing where the Bangkok Delight was located, they decided to take a leisurely walk to the restaurant and take the subway to return after dinner. Looking around and walking in a slow pace while enjoying fresh air and getting the mind away from all other considerations seemed so relaxing at the end of the day.

And they were sure to be mighty hungry after the walk by the time they reached the restaurant.

24

The weekend was generally a busy time for dinner at the restaurants around the University. However, Bangkok Delight was particularly popular because it not only had fancy Thai decorations in a tasteful arrangement giving the restaurant a cozy oriental atmosphere, but the menu was excellent and the service was superb. It was also smoke-free. Above all, it was not too expensive and they did not accept reservations. First come, first served was the policy. And when Lily and Samir arrived, they didn't have much of a wait to get seated.

No sooner did they get situated at the table than a cool glass of water with a slice of lemon was offered. "Nothing like a cool glass of water after a walk," Lily commented as she took a sip and started looking at the menu. Pretty soon the waiter came around and took their order. However, Samir still kept looking at the menu and it didn't take much effort for Lily to notice that Samir was plunged in some deep thought.

"Seems like something is bothering you, or something is brewing in your head. What's the matter, Samir?" Lily got a little worried thinking that Samir might be exhausted after the strenuous day.

"Oh, no, there's nothing wrong. I am sorry that I got lost for a moment in my thoughts. But no, there's no problem," Samir tried to reassure Lily as he smiled and softly touched her on the shoulder.

"I know better, Samir. You can't pretend. Tell me, what's wrong?"

"Well, to tell the truth, I do not like the idea that in the eyes of the world we are not a unity, that we are not a husband and wife. And I know that the fault is entirely mine. And that's what was troubling me."

"No, no, no! I don't find any fault if you wanted to make every effort for our wedding to be a family affair. That's what it's supposed to be; a joyous ceremonious union of two families. But if all our efforts fail and for whatever reason, whether because of customs, traditions, likes or dislikes, we are unable to soften the rigid attitudes, then there is nothing more we can do. And in that event my solution is quite simple. We arrange our own wedding and invite everyone in the families regardless of their approval or disapproval. If they join, so much the better. It will be fun. If not, we don't hold anything against anyone and just go on with our lives. Does that make sense to you?" Lily was quite at ease without getting perturbed as she laid out her thoughts in a casual matter of fact manner.

"O, I fully agree. That's why I said that the fault is entirely mine. I have really tried, Lily, but I find that the family positions are quite irreconcilable. My family wants a marriage within it's own orthodox faith and your family thinks that I am still in school and not gainfully employed. Hence, they are convinced that some `love-bug' must have gotten in your head to get engaged with a person like me without any source of steady income. After all, a man must be able to support a wife. And I cannot blame them if they do not approve of your getting married to me. I fully understand everyone's position. But having realized the reality, I should have gone ahead and planned our wedding a long time ago without waiting to see if given time the families would change their mind. And that's what was bothering me," Samir laid open his troubled feelings.

Just then the waiter arrived with a tray of dishes steaming hot with appetizing aroma. Arranging the dishes properly on the table, the waiter lit the candle and the dinner was served with a glass of house wine. But before beginning to eat, Samir lifted the wineglass and toasting with Lily he said, "Here's to our happy life," and with a sip of sparkling wine they began the dinner.

The food was prepared just right and as they were enjoying the delicious meal, Samir said: "You know what I propose to do now? Since your election to the parliament is set at the end of the coming month, and it will require our intense campaigning, I do not want a rush job of our wedding. But as soon as the election is over, we shall have a victory celebration galore: for your winning the election and my winning Lily! A double win! That's the plan. I tell you, it will be a blast."

"No doubt it will be marvelous. But it really doesn't matter when the wedding takes place, Samir. For a wedding after all is only a socio-cultural event structured into the social fabric for stable human relationship. All I know is that you are mine and I am yours forever. Even death shall not part us. It's the inviolable commitment, the indestructible bond and the immortal love that matters; the rest is inconsequential for me. True, the traditions and formalities have cultural value and social significance without which the whole institution of marriage and family would collapse. But if the basic sustaining element of abiding faith in inseparable unity weakens, whether for personal differences, individual worth and ambitions, personality conflicts, family feuds or for other considerations, then the sacrifice, the tolerance, the understanding and the accommodation of ego and personal feelings required in any lasting relationship begin to wear out and a whole chain of events ensues including separation, divorce, re-marriage and single parenting. Scientific knowledge, technology and new realities fostered by the age of "pills" are exploding the outmoded traditions, old taboos, myths and religious orthodoxy. Relationship between a man and a woman is viewed strictly a personal matter, no virtue being seen in refraining from nature's most pleasurable act. And some argue that the need for celibacy came about at a time when pregnancy was unavoidable. But in this age of techno-medical innovations, why risk temptations and perverted acts and go against the most powerful of innate human impulses and lead an unnatural life if it is not a compulsion or forced necessity, particularly when convenient and safe means of reproductive control are available? Seeking love, pleasure, enjoyment and gratification, here and now, appear so natural and seem to supersede hollow morality. Perhaps that's an inevitable change in the fast moving modern world of a new socio-economic outlook, propelled by technological advances, personal freedom and economic independence in an increasingly impersonal mega-city world of huge apartment complexes where nobody bothers who lives where and how! Be it as it may, Samir, the cultural values are fast changing and to some marriage is an outmoded bourgeois relic! But, in so far as I am concerned, whatever, whenever and howsoever you plan for the wedding is fine with me. I know everyone will have great fun in a 'winning celebration' as you put it."

"You don't know Lily how lonely I feel, how empty my life is without you. I need you Lily. I can't explain what it is, but your mere presence, your mere proximity, your just being there within the sphere of my eyesight breathes life into me. I just want you with me every moment of my life."

"So do I, Samir," and they both paused for a moment from the dinner and held each other's hand while looking into each other's smiling eyes.

And after finishing the dinner, without missing the special dessert of the evening, a light preparation made with fresh coconut milk, which they both relished, Lily and Samir returned to the University via the subway.

Samir left Lily at her home and headed straight to his room after a long heart felt embrace.

25

Samir wanted Lily's birthday to be a special occasion and when he found out that her parents would not participate if he were going to be present, he knew that Lily would be disheartened and saddened. Although Samir himself was also disappointed, he knew that that's the way the world is. Human behavior is not always rational. Perhaps, more often than not, it is reactive, prone to impulses and emotions and to irrational reflexes coupled with pre-conceived personal preferences, Samir thought. But, he did not wish to engage in analyzing human behavioral dynamics. And accepting things as they were he proceeded to make the best of the situation. He just wanted to make Lily as happy as he could.

It immediately occurred to Samir that Lily would be home and it will take away all the excitement of a birthday party if all preparations were made in her presence. So he called Meira Rosen and explaining to her the party plans, asked her to get Lily out on some pretext or the other so that while they were gone, he could get everything set and the party would be ready for a gala celebration by the time Meira and Lily returned.

In a few minutes Meira called back and indicated that Lily was on her way out to meet her and that Samir could go ahead with his plans safely.

It suddenly occurred to Samir that it would make Lily very happy and lift her spirits if Professor Watson showed up in the party. Of course, Professor Watson felt honored and enthused at being invited to join in this special birthday celebration for Lily when Samir called him. Professor Watson assured that he would be on time.

Samir invited a whole bunch of friends and acquaintances, both his and Lily's, for the party, requesting a couple of those with whom he was close to come a little early and help set up the place. The mere hint of celebrating Lily's birthday seemed to perk up Baba with unbound energy and he went around and decorated the dining room with balloons and other adornments that Samir had brought.

Pretty soon the punch, soda, snacks and all kinds of party platters got arranged on the dining table with a large chocolate cake at the center and the party was ready to commence at 3 p.m. The dining room got full with friends who arrived on time and as soon as Meira came in with Lily as planned at 3:10 p.m., the crowd cheered: "Happy Birthday to you. Happy Birthday to you. Happy birthday, dear Lily, Happy Birthday to you," as Lily blew the candle on the chocolate cake amid loud applause. Then, at that moment Professor Watson came forward from behind and hugged Lily wishing her many happy returns of the day.

Lily was surprised and overwhelmed seeing Professor Watson at the party and unable to hold back her joyous tears, she tried to smile while Dr. Watson gently held her lovingly.

Lily then cut the cake and Samir passed it around. Everybody was happy and enjoying the party, congratulating Lily and assuring her that they will pitch in and make her parliamentary campaign a grand success. Lily felt very happy at the affection and support she was receiving.

After a little while when everyone has had something to eat, Meira requested Ibrahim Suleman, an accomplished comic and lecturer in the Department of Drama & Theatrics at the University, to tell some of his politically incorrect jokes, which were particularly funny because of his deliberate Arab accent, keeping in mind, Meira reminded Ibrahim, that Lily was now a political candidate, although of a different kind!

Ibrahim's jokes made everybody turn over with laughter and people thoroughly enjoyed his banter, puns and skits.

And after a lot of fun, felicitations and merry making, the party concluded.

Everyone had a great time and Lily thanked everyone for coming and joining in the fun.

26

Most of Samir's data gathering, analyses and studies required for his doctoral degree were complete at the time Dr. Watson's shooting episode occurred. Realizing that Lily's parliamentary election would require his full attention, Samir devoted extra hours to give final touches to his dissertation and submitted it to the Advisory Committee for a *viva voce* in defense of his thesis. The Committee was very pleased with Samir's brilliant mathematical studies on the "Dynamics of Black Hole Formation" and voted unanimously for the grant of doctoral degree.

Lily was standing outside the Committee Room and congratulated Samir as he opened the door and came out with a broad smile on his face declaring: "I did it! The dissertation was accepted!"

Lily jumped with joy and felt mighty proud of Samir as she submitted herself to Samir's affectionate embrace.

The Department did not wish to lose such a promising scientist and offered him a teaching position as an Assistant Professor upon conferment of the doctoral degree. Samir was delighted at the offer and accepted it subject to his appointment commencing with the new academic year. Samir wanted to have absolutely unencumbered time to devote first to Lily's parliamentary election and then to a gala victory celebration together with a fabulous wedding ceremony. And then he planned to disappear with Lily for a momentous honeymoon in Kashmir after visiting the *Taj Mahal* as planned. Until then he did not wish to accept any appointment or burden of any kind and wanted to be totally free to celebrate and endear his marriage to Lily. "We live only once, Lily, and I want to cherish every moment of our being, of our togetherness," Samir said as he explained to Lily how he wanted to begin his career.

"I know how absorbed you get in whatever you undertake. So I think your plans fit your personality and I am looking forward to the days in Kashmir when I shall have the pleasure of having you full time by my side. Promise?" Lily looked at Samir with curious eyes.

"Promise!" Samir answered with a soft kiss on Lily's cheek.

"Then let's begin our election strategy so that we know exactly how, when and what we have to do. Remember, we have a well financed, powerful and politically well-connected lobby to reckon with," Lily was quite cognizant of the challenge.

"I know that, Lily, and it doesn't bother me a bit! In fact it may be to our advantage because people would love to defeat a behemoth! In any event, let me tell you how we should handle the campaign," Samir continued. "You know most people are at work during the day time. Therefore, we have to concentrate our campaign activities during the evening hours and over the weekend, leaving you absolutely free without any conflict to attend to your regular obligations and official duties at the University. Besides, the issues in this campaign are so very clear, so uncomplicated that, as I see it, all that is required to win is to get the message out. If the message reaches the people, they can make only one choice: not to get killed, intimidated, exploited, hurt, terrorized or abused by the gun-carrying inveterate individuals. So the work is pretty much cut out for us. Do you agree?"

"I do. But that's the rub. How do we get the message out? You are not thinking of buying time on TV, are you? Because I don't have to tell you that buying time on TV costs a huge amount of money and money corrupts both, the politics and the politician. And if you don't have your campaign chest full of money, you have no chance. You are lost in the wilderness. So what's the magic, Samir?" Lily was thinking loud.

"Money, power and politics! That's a separate, albeit quite relevant subject of enormous importance, particularly in a democratic set up. True, every individual seems to possess a sphere of power, the assertive dimension of which appears to extend from personal to geo-political, sometimes determining the course of history! And it needs no elaboration, Lily, that power breeds coercion. But we shall refrain from exploring the dynamics of power politics, leaving the enormously influential role of money for discussion by the entire new parliament where you, as a member, would be in a leading position to sort out this rather complicated and messy issue. But for now we shall adopt the true and tested classical campaign strategy of direct public involvement," Samir suggested.

"In fact I think direct public involvement will be a more effective campaign strategy than TV ads anyhow," Lily seemed confident in her views.

"Then we are all set," Samir concluded.

"Now then what we need to do next is to have a strategy session with all the group leaders of the student body so that we could have everyone's input in evolving a united and fully coordinated action plan for public involvement," Lily proposed.

"Absolutely correct," Samir readily concurred.

"Of course, arranging this strategy session is your job, my dear," Lily winked at Samir with a naughty look.

Samir was quick to respond, saying "May I, first, have a strategy session with you, Ma'am?" and he grabbed Lily into his arms.

"You are impatient, aren't you?" Lily was bashful.

"And you are eager, aren't you?" Samir retorted tightening his grip around Lily.

And with a bit of fun, play and pleasure, they proceeded to have dinner that Baba had prepared with so much care, not forgetting the special sweet dish that Samir so fondly enjoyed.

27

The next day Samir discussed the plan for a strategy session with all the group leaders of the student body and convened a meeting to arrive at a consensus plan of action.

John Hamilton from the School of Economics, Annie Lee Chung from the School of Liberal Arts, Meira Rosen from the School of Law, David Raymond from the School of Political Science and various other class representatives assembled at the conference room in the Student Union building.

Requesting the group to come to order, Samir asked Lily to open the discussion with a brief statement of purpose.

"I want to begin this discussion with two premises for the parliamentary campaign. First, there shall be no soft money or big campaign financing game. That's a part of the problem and we shall not be beholden to money." Everyone cheered as Lily spoke those words.

"Second, even though our public meetings and demonstrations may be spirited, enthusiastic and even overwhelming, we shall remain absolutely civil and maintain our dignity despite provocation, jeers or insults bound to come from our opponents. I realize it is a tall order. But the alternative is creation of confusion and misperception in the public mind and a discredit to our cause. Without being vain in any manner, I can only cite the dialectics of Gandhi who, as you know, with steadfast adherence to nonviolence and respect for the opponent, brought down the mighty British power to its knees! It was not easy and required great sacrifices, tolerance and perseverance. But it was also an unparalleled victory of principled struggle. I now invite your comments, thoughts and suggestions," Lily was somber as she concluded her remarks.

When, after waiting for a few moments, there were no comments, Samir asked the assembly: "Do I take it that all of us here agree with the discipline and steadfast determination required for this campaign? If yes, all say "Aye".

And there was an unanimous "Aye."

Then, expressing her deep gratification at the unity and manifest conviction of the group, Lily reported to the gathering that the large membership of WOFFL (Women for Fear-Free Living), a powerful civic organization, being very upset and distressed over recent rapes of two young women at gun point, passed an unanimous resolution endorsing our

"Ban the Gun" campaign and to participate in defeating the incumbents for the parliamentary election. WOFFL is of the view, Lily explained, that it is mostly, if not exclusively, men, not women, who are gun-possessors and there is no reason for the women to be the targets of their exploitation, violence, abuse and terror. Linda McMahon, President of WOFFL, got in touch with me," Lily continued, "and indicated that WOFFL will join forces with us and participate in the campaign."

"I am thrilled at this development. For let's face it, roughly half the population is women and WOFFL's deep anguish and expressed determination to actively participate in our campaign is a welcome news," Samir commented.

"Our strength is in numbers," Lily continued: "therefore, I propose a massive rally a week before election on Saturday morning at 10 O'clock at the Central Park with open public participation and attendance of WOFFL and the entire student body."

"I shall let WOFFL know of the date and time of the rally and it is now up to each one of us to spread the word around" Lily concluded her remarks.

"I know this will be an exciting story for the public media to cover and they will talk about it from morning till evening. You know how these commentators are. Each one wants to be the first to report the events and the news. So without spending a penny, there will be plenty of TV coverage," Samir confidently assured the gathering.

"Let's then marshal our strength and prepare for the rally," Samir proposed concluding the meeting and he thanked everyone for participating.

28

It was a gorgeous Saturday morning, sunny and bright with perfect 22°C weather. People started pouring in from all directions into Central Park right from nine O'clock and it was not very long before the entire park was full of people. The massive turnout for the rally was beyond expectation!

Just a few minutes before 10 O'clock, WOFFL president Linda McMahon, John Hamilton, Meira Rosen, Lily and Samir appeared on the dais followed by Dr. Watson who was brought to the high platform flanked by Annie Chung and David Raymond.

Precisely at 10 O'clock, Lily came forward to the microphone and addressing the gathering she said: "Good morning, ladies and gentlemen," and with a brief pause to let the gathering focus attention, she continued: "we have come together here at a historic moment to assert our right as citizens of a democratic country. Life under the fear of crime and violence is contrary to our fundamental freedoms and there is no place in a civil society for the sale of weapons of terror and murder. Shooting and killing, rape and intimidation have become an every day affair and we, as a people, must now rise to eradicate what the politicians and the legislature refuse to do under the influence of power politics and big money lobby." Then with a momentary pause to attract peoples' attention and raising her hand, Lily asked with a loud voice: "Are we ready?" and the entire mass responded with one thunderous clamor of "Y...e...s" filling the whole sky!

"Although still a little weak from the gunshot wounds, he insisted to be with all of us at this gathering. So, ladies and gentlemen, here is Professor Watson," so saying Lily moved aside for Dr. Watson to come forward to the microphone. And as Dr. Watson came forward, the entire crowd greeted him with lengthy applause.

Wishing to express his feelings Dr. Watson waved with both hands and standing at the microphone acknowledged to the people: "Thank you ladies and gentlemen for your warm affection. I am deeply touched. But isn't it peculiar that the gunman wanted me to be dead but miraculously I am alive! Perhaps I was destined to survive for a different cause! Be it as it may, the result is that an encounter with death has liberated my spirit. I am now free and fearless. I shall march with you to the Parliament House and we shall let the power-hungry, self-serving politicians know that their days are numbered. And we, the people, exercising our legitimate right of franchise, shall throw out the incumbents and there shall be no possession, ownership or sale of murderous weapons anymore! Freedom now, freedom at last, freedom at last!” announced Dr. Watson amid loud cheers from the masses as he spoke those words.

“Let’s march together, hand in hand. And let not the politicians’ design but the people’s power prevail! And all in agreement say a loud `Aye’,” Dr. Watson asked. And a thunderous `A...y...e’ filled the sky!

“Let me now yield to Linda McMahon, President of WOFFL, to give you directions how our rally shall march and how we will all proceed.” Dr. Watson then moved aside allowing WOFFL president Linda McMahon to come to the microphone.

“I am thrilled to see you all excited in our united purpose for a fearless living, for feeling secure in conducting our daily lives without dreading violence. It’s a minimum requirement of a civil society. Let me tell you, there is no reason to have an industry that manufactures and sells deadly means of violence to the public. This high profit business has controlled the politicians through huge soft money contributions and the time has come to root out the cause, to ban the public sale, possession or use of murderous weapons: pistols, guns, rifles and firearms.”

“The purpose of this rally and the march is to

demonstrate to the world that we the people do have the power to alter even a deeply entrenched system that the professional politicians refuse to change in their design to perpetuate and preserve their own place and power. Please remember that while our slogan shall be loud and clear, our march shall be absolutely peaceful. Let's not be surprised if the opponents attempt clever and covert means to provoke, incite or create disturbance and then blame it on us to discredit our cause! So let's be cautious, vigilant and resolute in our peaceful purpose."

"Lily and Dr. Watson have chosen to be at the front line in the center of the procession and we shall all follow hand-in-hand singing our slogans walking through the entire downtown and the business district. Finally, we shall assemble at the parade ground in front of the Parliament House where we will submit a memorandum of our demand to the Speaker of the House, if he desires to meet with us. If not, we shall leave the memorandum with the guard to deliver it to the Speaker and we shall then calmly disperse. So let's proceed."

And the march began.

29

As the procession proceeded from the Central Park and passed through the city streets, the shopkeepers and other businesses *en route* waved and cheered the marchers as they sang in chorus:

> *"Hey, Politicians! Hey, Politicians!*
> *Ban the Gun, Or, You Will Run!*
> *Do It Now, Do It Fast, Or, rest assured,*
> *You'll be Lost!"*

People were all excited and enthused as they repeated the slogan and the number of participants kept increasing as the march progressed. Some, who weren't sure about the kind of rally and demonstration it was, joined in as they witnessed the nature and purpose of the march. And by the time the procession passed through downtown, the number seemed to have tripled from the original gathering at the Central Park!

The procession progressed smoothly until it reached a cross-section leading to the street toward the Parliament House, when a man suddenly approached the procession from the opposite side and there suddenly occurred a loud explosion with a tremendous flash of light! A big bang with all sorts of scattered human fragments flying up in the air!

The frightened mass started screaming and running in every direction seeking safety and the entire procession turned into an utter confusion and chaos. The police, who were following the procession, swiftly moved in and tried to calm down the people in an effort to control the situation, while fire fighters and thc ambulance quickly appeared at the scene with sirens blowing. The area was swiftly cordoned off and the wounded rushed to the hospital. Several persons were found dead and the bodies removed to the morgue for identification and disposal by the Coroner's office under forensic procedures. Police picked up pieces of flesh and body parts from the bloodied scene to ensure proper identification of the shattered dead bodies.

From all indications, it appeared to be a case of suicide bombing.

Apart from the bomber, Dr. Watson was among those who did not survive the blast. Although it seemed that Lily was expected to be blown off as well, miraculously the blast resulted only in Lily being thrown off to the roadside with one of her legs torn off and hanging loose from the knee joint! Even though breathing, she was found unconscious and removed to the hospital with several bloody percussion to her body. It was reported that she was undergoing emergency surgery in an effort to join her severed leg. Many others were severely injured and receiving treatment at the hospital. The emergency room was full of wounded bodies.

It was an unimaginable scene of horror and pain and the entire city was in disbelief and sorrow.

30

The news of Dr. Watson's killing and Lily's hospitalization in an unconscious state spread swiftly and people's eyes were glued to the TV for further reports and developments. Hospital bulletins indicated that Lily's condition was critical; her severed leg couldn't be saved and had to be amputated.

All classes at the University remained suspended and there was an eerie silence throughout the campus, Dr. Watson's body having been placed for viewing at the center of the huge student union auditorium.

For three continuous days people poured in from morning till night in an incessant flow, patiently taking turn to place a bouquet of flowers at the open casket of this unusual scientist. As they passed by to pay their last respect, some simply looked at the casket in somber silence, some couldn't hold their tears, some knelt down and crossed their heart, and some simply shook their head perhaps in disbelief as to how this man of forthright reason could be so oblivious of reality! Or, was he so convinced of reason to prevail that he dismissed the reality? From the expression on their faces, it appeared that people just didn't understand why this had to happen and they wondered in vain.

Meanwhile, the University deliberated and reached the decision that apart from being an ingenious and brilliantly visionary scientist, he was a man of such extraordinary attributes, humility and courage that his body shall be buried in the ground in front of the Genetic Engineering Building where Dr. Watson devoted his life, had his laboratory and pursued his research tirelessly and that a full size statue of Dr. Watson shall be installed at the burial site.

It seemed a bit odd and ironic that sometimes it is death that brings immortality!

31

Although still in deep pain from trauma, wounds, and surgery, Lily had gained consciousness and begun to inquire about the incident and the condition of many who were with her at the rally and in the march, particularly about Samir and Dr. Watson. When she was told that Samir had suffered multiple severe concussions and head injuries from which he was recovering satisfactorily, but that Dr.

Watson was killed, Lily began to cry profusely unable to stop sobbing. The attending physicians and nurses tried to console her but her indescribable anguish was quite evident from the swollen reddened eyes. However, when she finally gained composure, she wanted to know where Samir was and when Dr. Watson's funeral was going to take place? And she wanted to know whether she could be allowed to see and touch Dr. Watson's body before the casket was lowered? And as she asked that question, she began to cry again. The staff promised to let her know whether and how she could do so.

The University decided to have Dr. Watson's burial on Sunday at high noon. The sky was clear, the sun was bright and there was a mild breeze blowing as if the Heavens had made special arrangement to accept this parted soul in its Kingdom with dignity. The entire University ground was full of students, faculty, staff, dignitaries and friends, all gathered to bid final good-bye to their beloved professor, colleague and fellow researcher.

Lily was brought in by an ambulance, and just as the pallbearers were ready to lower the casket, she got up on the crutches helped by Samir, came forward a few steps, kissed the casket and limped back with her head bowed.

As far as it could be seen, tears were rolling down each and every eye and people were holding each other's hand in consolation. This is all that Dr. Watson had as a family, if it could be called that! For he was an escapee immigrant from a distant land ravaged by war and atrocities and he did not know what had happened to his parents and family. Indeed, whenever he thought of his family, he was filled with grief in his heart as he tried to analyze how humans so blindly followed what they called as their "faith," "belief" or "religion," converting, proselytizing or subjugating people, waging wars and killing fellow humans while feeling righteous at the same time! Though unbelievable, he found it unsettling that killing of more humans was brought about by adherents of fundamental beliefs and edicts of 'Merciful' religions than by other causes!

The politics of religion and the influential sway of astute representatives of God, charming the humble and faithful with their exalted status and eloquent sermons, while leading a glorified life with large sums of money treasured and collected in the name of 'Almighty,' intrigued Dr. Watson and he often wondered whether the creative and self-righteous, the intelligent and ingenious, the shrewd and powerful didn't take advantage of the simple and unassuming? Whether people weren't influenced by their sense of loyal obedience and lured away by their emotional needs with intuitive feelings, rather than persuaded by reasoned rationality? He was amused, sometimes amazed, at the skillful organization of institutionalized hierarchical orders under the authoritative control of titular heads imposing peremptory loyalty, reverence and obedience on its faithful rank and followers as an abiding providential command! He found it equally fascinating that human frailties fervently yearning for solace, inner peace, and need for emotional support, had rendered preaching a powerful, prestigious and preferable profession by those who wished to perpetuate it! The study of theocracy and the workings of metaphysical organized establishments were interesting subjects for Dr. Watson to ponder and analyze.

But he never could understand why his innocent family was wiped out. Perhaps it was this episode which singularly left a deep scar and imprint on his mind as he shaped his life.

It was perhaps this adversity, which made him determined to succeed, never losing hope, always being industrious, humble and decisive. Even though alone, he never felt lonely. For he saw that the unraveling of the human genome had bestowed upon men the biological secret of evolution to *Homo sapiens*. And the fascination of bioengineering and research into genomics subsumed his entire energy even though he knew that at the practical level people carried on their lives in a normal manner, choosing their mating partner through traditional ways or by independent choice and recombination and assortment of genes was far from their mind. Leaving biology in whatever way it worked and unconcerned whether the ultimate design of 'Nature' was the production of gametes to reproduce, preserve and perpetuate the evolutionary progression of its species, people just seemed to engage in whatever came naturally to them, being more concerned with earning a living, raising and providing for the family, and seeking simple pleasures of life than thinking about mechanisms of gene action. But that was not the modality of an academic whose life was intertwined with scientific inquiry.

The more he learned of the mechanisms that control and regulate gene function beginning from the DNA to the proteins, to cells, tissues and organs through growth, development and senescence, the more he got absorbed in studying and delineating the step-by-step process. And one of the tools he used in his studies was that of genetic engineering. He was so excited with the potential of this revolutionary frontier of molecular biology coupled with nanotechnology that his enthusiasm and devotion touched every fellow in his laboratory and they pursued research with equal zeal, vigor and creativity. Indeed, to be working in Dr. Watson's lab was considered a privilege and honor by the student body.

Dr. Watson was happy and content with his work; his laboratory having been recognized as the premier center for advanced genomic research. Although self-made, and maybe because of it, Dr. Watson was quite modest, unpretentious and unassuming, a peculiar blend of an intellectual, visionary, and a simple human being. Perhaps this was all that this dedicated scientist was and maybe this was why he was so adored, loved and cherished.

He was unique in his own ways!

32

Lily slowly recovered and having lost one of her legs, she moved around either in a wheel chair or on crutches. She had to wait until the wound completely healed to receive an artificial limb. But she had no rancor for her condition and adjusted remarkably well to the new routine. Samir would try to help her, but he soon realized that Lily was happier doing her own thing. This is how perhaps all self-reliant people feel, Samir quickly came to understand.

Dr. Watson had become a father figure for Lily and his cruel killing, among many others whom she came to endear so much, seemed to have left a deep scar in her heart. This made Lily doubly determined to campaign with every breath of her soul for the parliamentary election, which was now just around the corner.

Lily and Samir took a few days' leave of absence from the University to devote full time for the campaign.

And as a part of her people-oriented strategy, Lily had Samir prepare a prominent message poster, which read as follows:

"I AM A LIVING RELIC OF MODERN CULTURE OF VIOLENCE. GIVE ME YOUR MANDATE AND AS A FIRST STEP, I WILL INTRODUCE LEGISLATION TO OUTLAW THE USE, POSSESSION, MANUFACTURE AND SALE OF ALL VARIETIES OF WEAPONS AND FIREARMS OF MURDER, TORTURE AND TERROR FROM OUR CIVILIZED SOCIETY."

"DEFEAT THOSE, WHO OPPOSE." — *Lily.*

All day long Lily held the poster by her side while sitting down in the wheel chair at a prominently conspicuous spot by the busy roadside so that every passerby could see her. When the traffic got hectic or busy, she would stand up in her crutches and wave at the people. They seemed to recognize her and wave back with a smile and enthusiastic acknowledgment. Those in a motor vehicle would honk and wave their hands through the window expressing their support.

The turnout for voting was overwhelming and Lily handily won the election with a landslide. The incumbents, even though supported by big money machine, got squarely rejected by the majority. It seemed that the people had spoken with an unmistakable voice. The defeat of the incumbents seemed to send a clear message to the lawmakers that the power of money, influence peddling and lobbying in politics had to be checked if true democracy serving peoples' interest, not the politicians' purpose, were to prevail.

A new parliament session was ready to convene.

33

Samir was ecstatic that the campaign being over, he was now able to arrange for a gala wedding ceremony coupled with celebration for Lily's election victory. He was of the view, however, that given all that had happened, those who knew Lily closely would be delighted to have the opportunity to participate in felicitating Lily's wedding and election victory. Hence, even if it seemed unconventional, Samir wanted the festivities not to be private but to be an open public affair for all those who wished to rejoice in the celebrations and ceremonies.

And then Samir planned to take off with Lily to a fabulous honeymoon.

Lily's wound had healed and using latest prosthetics the medical team performed an extraordinary feat in attaching an artificial limb to her severed leg so that her gait had returned to be unnoticeably natural. She carried herself with utmost confidence and dignity. Nevertheless, Samir knew that crippled with injury Lily would never be able to stand and walk unaided without the prosthetics. But for him this was entirely inconsequential. For Lily had become a part of his soul and inseparable from his being. Her existence had merged into his and nothing else mattered.

Marriage was now only a formality, albeit an important one of great social value and tradition, Samir recognized. However, the mere thought of a grand wedding ceremony thrilled Samir and he made detailed plans in his own mind how he would manage a large gathering of family, friends and fans, without giving any clue to Lily. Somehow he reveled and found great joy in surprising Lily.

Samir knew that Lily's folks weren't quite happy about Lily's relationship with him and his father wasn't quite prepared to accept Lily as his daughter-in-law. Given the unaccommodating strong feelings of both sides of the family, Samir didn't think it wise to raise the issue of marriage with either side, lest there be fresh contentions and hurt feelings. Hence, he thought it best to avoid any possibility of friction and made all arrangements for the ceremonies independently, simply informing and sending an invitation to everyone in the families seeking their blessing.

Somehow he hoped that the sheer news of marriage would instill instant excitement in the families and past resentments would fade away. He so much wished that they would all attend the ceremonies.

For the wedding and reception Samir selected *Imperial Garden*, a nineteenth century castle elaborately built of choice natural pink marbles, surrounded on all sides by colorful flower gardens, some with exotic fragrant blooms amid cool fountains.

The castle had been furnished with the most elegant appointments and facilities for banquet and entertainment. It provided just the kind of marvelous setting Samir envisioned for the gala festivities. It had a huge stage for dance and performance with superb acoustics for musical presentations. The attached dining hall sparkled with hand-crafted chandeliers of extraordinary designs and the layout was open enough to allow a cool breeze laden with the aroma of evening blooms to permeate gently through the halls.

Samir wanted this occasion to be as gorgeous as Lily was, as if to compensate for whatever Lily may have suffered and lost.

34

For the wedding, Samir ordered a special *Kashmiri* dress for Lily: a full length *kamiz,* ankle length free flowing *ghaghra* and *hijab,* a long wide scarf for head cover, all hand-woven in fancy golden embroidered silk with elegant matching floral prints for which Kashmir was especially renowned.

A magnificently matching set of diamond-ruby earrings, necklace and delicate bracelets was brought from *Istanbul* by Samir's aunt, *Hasina,* who was younger than Samir's mom but with whom Samir had spent much of his childhood. Samir was special to her and nothing could have held her back from attending Samir's marriage. Indeed, getting Lily all dressed up and adorned for the wedding and all similar details were left entirely with the aunt so that Samir could be absolutely assured that all bridal arrangements and preparations were elaborate and attended to in every minute detail with ambiance, elegance, funfair and festivities.

It was a pleasant surprise that the moment Samir introduced aunt Hasina, Lily found herself all wrapped up in aunt's bosom with her head suddenly resting on Hasina's shoulder, both of them somehow instinctively holding each other within their folded arms. It appeared as though Lily had found an incessant flow of unbound love in the tears suddenly rolling down aunt Hasina's smiling face. It was mysterious how such affection emanated so spontaneously, as if they had known and missed each other for ages! It was inexplicable why happiness brings out tears and how love and affection transcend all differences, reasons and rationality.

Aunt Hasina wanted to do everything for the bride-to-be that Samir's mom, and her late sister, would have done.

She wanted to adore her, adorn her, pamper her and feed her with her own hands with all sorts of sweets that she prepared herself. And she would dress up Lily in different styles of traditional attires required of a bride at different occasions: breakfast, lunch, dinner and dance.

Aunt Hasina thought of everything, made all preparations and was simply overjoyed finding Lily so affectionate, accommodating and adoptive.

And the evening before the wedding day aunt Hasina decorated Lily's palms, finger tips and toes with *Mehndi*, a traditional custom whereby the herbal *Mehndi* is artistically laid and allowed to develop overnight into magnificently colorful bright orange-red designs, a symbol of beauty and auspicious omen for a bride-to-be.

Lily was overwhelmed with all the unexpected, albeit affectionate, attention she was receiving from a person whom she never knew before. Lily's happiness was unbound and she felt most at ease and secure in aunt Hasina's companionship. Spontaneity of unpretentious affection seemed to transcend all cultural differences.

Elaborate arrangements were made at the *Imperial Garden* to accommodate a large gathering, which Samir anticipated for the dual celebration of Lily's wedding and successful election. Many, including the University faculty, staff and others who so fondly attended the Sunday Evening Forum, were expected to participate.

Several stalls of all varieties of exotic gourmet snacks, soft drinks, ice-cold *kevda-flavored-mango-lassi*, which Samir knew would be an especially enjoyable novelty for many a guest, were decoratively set under the shade of majestic trees throughout the Imperial Garden so that the guests could roam around, mingle and have fun prior to the formal wedding ceremony scheduled to take place exactly at *go-dhooli* (dusk), which aunt Hasina believed to be an auspicious moment. And Samir couldn't ignore this singular wish of his beloved aunt even if he thought astrological beliefs to be occult. Lily was analytical but understanding in her approach. Consequently, she had no preference of any kind in these mundane matters, feeling quite comfortable and content with whatever made aunt Hasina and Samir happy. To her, happiness was more important than fussing over trivia.

So at dusk everyone gathered around the wide-open stretch of lush green lawn at the center of the Imperial Garden in front of the majestic castle, where a decorated *mandap* (platform) was temporarily erected for the performance of wedding rituals by a *Vedic* priest who was especially invited for the occasion. Although Samir didn't subscribe to *Vedic* beliefs, he was nevertheless enchanted by the ceremonies of *Vedic* tradition whereby the bride and the groom were united in holy matrimony under the sanctity of Sacred Fire, a symbol of purity and universal energy.

Samir wanted something distinctive for the wedding ceremonies and the concept behind the *Vedic* rituals simply fascinated him.

The guests watched the ceremonies with great interest when the priest, reciting *Vedic mantras*, enunciated the vows that the bride and groom solemnly exchanged by bowing to the priest, the guests being revered witness to the holy matrimony. The newlyweds then together performed one rotation circling the Sacred Fire in solemn acknowledgment of their faithful commitment in holy matrimony and the guests then showered the couple with flowers, thereby concluding the matrimonial formalities.

Samir and Lily had hoped that their parents would join in the celebrations and bless the couple. But it didn't happen!

Lily looked most elegant in the *Kashmiri* wedding outfit adorned with sparkling diamond-ruby earrings, necklace and bracelets that aunt Hasina had brought. She was a perfect picture of joy and happiness, embracing everyone who came to congratulate her.

The newlyweds and the guests then moved inside the dazzling castle richly decorated and brightly lit, where a sumptuous dinner was arranged while on the stage a live orchestra played melodious tunes befitting the occasion.

After the dinner the newlyweds were toasted by the President of the University and hearty congratulations were extended to Lily for her election to the Parliament amid tumultuous cheers echoing: "We Love Lily, We Love Lily!"

Deeply moved by the outpouring of such affection, Lily stood and bowed to the assembled guests.

The newlyweds then cut the cake while the live band struck the dancing tune, whereupon Samir gently held Lily with his folded arms and led her to the center of the hall for a slow dance. Lily gracefully cooperated with a few steps. But then the guests took over and danced, and danced, and danced!

Everyone was having great fun and enjoying the festivities with desserts, *pistachio-falooda-kulfi*, fruits, cake, coffee, tea and various assortments of other sweet delicacies arranged all round the dance hall for the guests.

The flower gardens outside were glowing majestically under the soothing reflection of the moonlit sky filled with the twinkling stars. It was a perfect evening for a stroll through the gardens. The mild breeze laden with the fragrance of blooming Jasmines felt especially delightful as the guests dispersed from the castle through the garden after dessert and dance.

The "Imperial Suite" on the upper floor of the castle was especially reserved for the newlyweds. During refurbishing of the castle all peripheral walls on this floor were replaced with reflective tinted glass, which was completely opaque from the outside but transparent from the inside. Elegant draperies were hung on mechanized bars all round the suite so that the curtains could be opened or closed, partially or completely, at will by remote sensors depending on the mood and the particular view desired. The suite was luxuriously furnished with all amenities so that the couple could have a thrilling and romantic wedding night.

The silvery moonlit night was young and the quiet serenity of the garden was irresistible for the newlyweds to retire in each other's warm embrace.

They were ready to take off for their honeymoon the next day.

35

Samir vividly remembered Lily's honeymoon wishes of visiting the *Taj Mahal* at midnight during full moon and sailing on the *houseboat* in the pristine lakes of Kashmir known for their grandeur under the shadow of surrounding mountain ranges. Therefore, as a part of planning marriage celebrations, Samir also made a detailed itinerary for their arrival, the day after the wedding, first at the *Taj Mahal* and then at Kashmir. He confirmed the flight reservations and carefully made all travel arrangements so that Lily would have a fabulous journey with ease and comfort.

Although regarded as one of the most beautiful

structures in the world, the *Taj Mahal* assumes special elegance under the glow of full moon shining on the pure white *Makrana* marbles of the domes and slender minarets, all elegantly reflected in the sparkling clear water of its central pool. Surrounding this majestic marble pool were beautiful gardens with well placed dark green cypress trees in the background at the periphery of the grounds. This monument of magnificence and grandeur memorializes unbound love of an emperor for his devoted queen and Lily wished to commemorate the first night of her honeymoon at this landmark.

Arriving during the day, Lily and Samir spent hours looking awe-struck at the design, architecture and precious stone laden decorative motifs of the mausoleum, which is so situated on the banks of the river *Yamuna* that it can be seen across a bend in the river from the Emperor's palace only a short distance away. The Emperor was so grief stricken with the loss of his beloved wife that he just wanted to have the tomb within his eyesight from the palace. Such was his love.

And when the Emperor died, he was buried, as he had wished, next to his wife in the mausoleum, which was called '*Taj Mahal*" after his wife's name *Mumtaz*.

Lily and Samir returned to the *Taj Mahal* again at midnight when the bright full moon was straight up at the zenith glistening on this monument with unparalleled splendor. Lily didn't know how or why, but at this magnificent *Mazaar* and sight of radiant glory she couldn't help feeling that it is only love that was precious, perpetual and intransient. That love lasted longer than time. And even though entirely inexplicable, somehow she felt at that moment that Samir was the essence of her 'being'. And she reflexively held Samir tight, embracing him to her heart with an expression of immense fulfillment and satiation, which was indescribable.

Samir immediately folded Lily into his arms and gently kissed her.

Then they leisurely strolled to the hotel while imbibing the serene glory of the midnight sky shining softly in the radiance of the silvery moon.

It was a memorable evening.

36

The next day they arrived at Srinagar to begin exploring the fabled *Valley of Kashmir*.

This valley of unequalled natural beauty, grandeur and scenery at the foothills of the Himalayan ranges, has ever been a land of poetic interlude and romantic fascination. And for a life to be lived only once, Lily wanted to adore and enjoy every moment of it.

Samir was equally imaginative and selected a houseboat on the silky waters of *Dal Lake* in the seclusion of the lake interior.

There were several hawkers all around the lake-rim displaying exquisite silk garments, shawls, woolen sweaters and various handicraft items of Kashmir fame. They easily discerned vacationers from the native visitors and tried to attract them to the merchandise. Fascinated vacationers were a good source of profit. Novelty of fine Kashmiri artwork enchanted curious visitors and they always paid more! No matter how cleverly one tried, these hawkers couldn't be outsmarted in bargaining. Haggling was nevertheless a lot of fun and the customer felt happy purchasing an item for Rs. 20 when the price quoted was Rs. 200! The amusing part was that despite such disparate pricing, thc mcrchant still felt happy that he made a sale with profit! Bargaining was nevertheless in good zest with lots of fun and smiles all over.

Samir had fanciful ideas about Lily's clothing during the honeymoon. And he knew that it was the revelation of the unexpected and the element of spontaneous surprise that added to the excitement of anticipation. Hence, while Lily was examining the exquisite hand-woven embroidered Kashmiri shawls of unmatched designs so soft to the touch and considered purchasing one, Samir picked up some fine pure white Kashmir silk garments of exotic styles and transparency. Mere imagination of how Lily would look in these intimate clothing was quietly sensitizing Samir and he was eager to get settled in the houseboat.

Built of cedar wood the houseboat was beautifully decorated with adjustable curtains and furnished with all amenities so much so that the guests need not leave this comfortable floating facility for any purpose whatsoever if they didn't want to! Breakfast, lunch and dinner were prepared fresh onboard by a gourmet cook at the pleasure of the visitors and served at hours preferred by them. Special tea, and more tea, was served whenever desired. The visitors were otherwise left alone undisturbed, the attendant-cook leaving in his *Shikara* after tidying up the kitchenette.

A hand pedaled gondola, *Shikara*, was the only means of moving to and from the houseboat and it was simply relaxing to glide with the *Shikara* on the placid waters in the warmth of late afternoon, touching the soft white and pink petals of innumerable lotus flowers spread all over the lake with their silken dark green glistening sepals floating on the water. Lily and Samir had conjured up their own secret plans in anticipation of this secluded *Shikara* excursion on the lake, both of them having their own amorous designs in their mind.

As Samir leisurely maneuvered the *Shikara* through the scattered rows of lovely lotus flowers, pretty soon they were deep inside the interior of the lake feeling the soothing touch of mild mountain breeze and marveling the majesty of the valley. But Lily felt a bit warm and took off the formal gown laying it aside in a corner, only the pure white translucent half-sleeve short silk *Kamiz (Chemise)* underneath now adorning this youthful bride. The soft silken *Kamiz* was so thin, supple and pliant that it adhered to every contour of Lily's attractive body revealing the engorged curvatures with clear prominence. And she intentionally drew closer to Samir, as close as she could, in a veiled attempt to take the paddle from him as if to try her hand at steering the *Shikara*. But just as she really intended, it was natural and unavoidable for Samir to notice the allure of Lily's inviting exuberant body, secretly but irresistibly instilling in him an innate longing and desire. Nature seems to have evolved the charming beauty of undisguised youthful breasts in such a manner as to entice magical male attraction and courtship leading to playful mating of such immense joy as to trigger a longing for repeated indulgence. For it served Nature's purpose of perpetuating multiplication and evolution of its species. Whatever it may be, it was inevitable that Samir felt the sensual touch of Lily's warm body as she drew closer and the sensation of this close encounter stirred something instinctive within him, which was sensual and irrepressible. And with a whispering soft voice he said to Lily: "You want me Lily, don't you?"

"And just the two of us in this lovely valley, don't you need me, Samir?" Lily responded with the touch of her moist lips coupled with an irresistible embrace. And with playful passionate caressing, they grew eager and impatient enjoying each other with intense pleasure and sensuality culminating in fulfilling relaxation while the *Shikara* silently floated in the open solitude of the lake.

The cool breeze over the lake felt invigorating and they returned to the houseboat for afternoon tea; this time Lily really trying her hand at paddling the *Shikara*.

The lake was usually calm in the evening and surrounded by luxuriant *Chinar* groves in the background, the myriad majestic colors of sunset reflected with startling clarity in the water under the shadow of the mountains. It was a picture of breathtaking magnificence and the lake whispered in unison with the lucid notes of *bulbul* and *kokil* returning to their nests. The sunset on the lake was particularly spectacular and Lily and Samir tried to imbibe the splendor of this evening glory in their mind's eye so that it would remain eternally indelible.

The chef had prepared a special Kashmiri dinner, *Wazwaan*, and both of them relished it with great satisfaction in candlelight while the lake sparkled under the brightness of the moonlit sky.

They were then left alone to retire for the night in the

quiet coziness of the houseboat with an enchanting view of the vast expanse of the sleeping valley in silent slumber of twinkling stars.

37

The next day Lily and Samir visited the *Shalimar* gardens, a legendary monument of love and romance bordering the lake. Panoramic elegance of the valley and its cool climate were so pleasing that this magnificent garden of unmatched beauty beneath the overspread of snow-covered mountaintops was artistically laid out by romantic *Mughal* emperors for sheer pleasure and relaxation. Such was their view of life.

Shaded by royal tall *Chinars*, the trees of exquisite splendor majestically surrounding the entire landscape, the fragrance of myriad rare and colorful flowers flooded the *Shalimar*. Radiating waterways and springing fountains dividing a series of flower terraces added grandeur to the glory of the garden. Legend had it that it was in these gardens that Emperor *Jahangir* relaxed and celebrated life with his beautiful bride *Noorjahan* amid the sweet smell of a thousand roses!

Neither Samir nor Lily knew how or why such legends remain memorable and why the sight of lakes, flowers and mountains invariably rouse romantic notion? All that Lily wished, though, as she visited these timeless monuments, was the endowment of love.

Love.

Nothing but love.

That's all Lily wanted!

Life without love seemed an empty dream, an unnatural existence, a play without a song!

And Samir's caring adoration filled with the purity of intense affection was more than anything else Lily could desire.

Although a thoughtful analytical outlook was so natural for science-oriented Samir and Lily, it was perhaps these tender moments that made it comprehensible for them that apart from the intellectual dimension of reason and rationality, there was another qualitative dimension relating to the intensity of deep inner feelings that created the *Taj Mahal* and *Shalimar*. And perhaps it was this experience of the visceral, tender, and subtle that created the art, the literature and the music. And it was the lyrics of life that lived as poems. And perhaps it was these expressions of human feelings and emotions, of human dreams and desires that formed the cultural heritage so guardedly cherished by humanity from generation to generation. While science explored the true nature of things and refined knowledge, it was affection, compassion, song and beauty that gave meaning to existence and enriched life, they came to understand.

But for the moment they found all this dialectic out of place and irrelevant. They just wanted to feel the fascination and lore of *Shalimar*, the garden where *Jahangir* and *Noorjahan* celebrated their love in an eternal honeymoon.

So they simply held each other's hand and looked at each other with a silent expression of mysterious fulfillment, which was entirely inexplicable as they strolled through the majestic flower-laden terraces of *Shalimar* overflowing with the alluring aroma of innumerable pink, yellow and red roses, before returning to their houseboat for the journey back home.

38

Returning home, Samir picked up the morning paper and noticed that the police had identified a group suspected to be involved in the bomb explosion as well as in the firing of gunshots targeting Dr. Watson after his lecture at the Sunday Evening Forum. Samir immediately turned on the TV to learn the latest on this news report, but all that he could gather was that the police were very cautious in discussing any details with the public media because of the sensitivity of the matter!

Lily wanted to wait and see the evidence before

thinking any more on the issue, although she was gratified that at least there seemed to be something, rather than nothing, in these sensational investigative reports.

A preliminary hearing was scheduled at the courthouse the next morning.

Sharply at 9 a.m., Judge Hamid entered the court through the side door and the bailiff yelled: "All rise! Honorable Judge Yosef Hamid presiding."

Everyone got up from the seat.

"Good morning, ladies and gentlemen! Please be seated," said the Judge as he stepped up to the bench and took the high-back, leather-upholstered swivel chair.

"Please call the first case," the Judge said as he looked at the clerk.

"State versus Donald Hamilton and Robert Christian," shouted the clerk.

Just then the bailiff handed over a piece of paper to the Judge.

"What's this?"

"A petition for live transmission of the proceedings via cable-TV, Your Honor."

"What?"

"Yes, Your Honor! Because of great public interest in this case, the media wish to record and relay the proceedings live."

Adjusting his bifocal glasses Judge Hamid looked

penetratingly at the TV crew assembled at the rear of the court room and said: "This is not a soap-opera for entertainment of the public. Neither is the courtroom a forum for theatrics, attorney drama or glorification. It is a hall for serious deliberations and justice under the law, which is often better served, not with, but without publicity."

And then, picking up the pen to write something, the Judge continued: "Petition denied. Please clear the court room quickly of all cameras and recording devices of any kind whatsoever."

All eyes looked back at the media crew as they began moving out of the courtroom.

"Are the counsels ready? The witnesses here?" the Judge inquired.

The prosecutor and the defense attorney seated at the front row near the bench nodded their head.

"Very well. As you all know this is only a preliminary hearing, not a trial. The purpose of a preliminary hearing is to determine whether there is sufficient cause to send the case to the grand jury. The defendants have the right, of course, to waive the preliminary hearing if they so choose. If not, based on the sufficiency of evidence showing a crime has been committed, the defendants could be bound over to the grand jury," deliberated the Judge.

More often than not, a preliminary hearing provides

the defense some measure of the weight of evidence relied upon by the prosecution against the defendants. Hence, it is rare, if ever, that the preliminary hearing is waived.

Defense Counsel Eric Lumumba then immediately got up and said: “No, Your Honor! We do not intend to waive the preliminary hearing.”

The Judge then, looking at the affidavit of Detective Golden charging both defendants of conspiracy, aggravated assault and attempted murder of Dr. Watson, turned to the State’s Attorney Philip Long and instructed: "If the State is ready, please call your first witness.”

“The State calls Detective Golden, Your Honor.”

Detective Robert Golden was sworn and seated at the witness chair.

“Please state your full name.”

“Robert Golden, Chief Detective for the Criminal Investigation Division of Ocean City Police Department.”

“How long have you served the police department in this capacity?”

“For more than eleven years.”

“In your affidavit to the Court, you have charged the defendants with conspiracy, aggravated assault and attempted murder, is that correct?”

“Yes.”

“Please tell the Court what you base your charges on.”

“As soon as the news flashed on the TV reporting Dr.

Watson having been shot at the University Sunday Evening Forum and the police requested any information leading to the apprehension or arrest of the assailants who had cleverly escaped the scene, our hotline started ringing off the hook with all kinds of leads about the suspects. All incoming information was carefully recorded and we started investigating the leads."

"What happened then?"

"One informant seemed to have noticed a group of people huddling and hiding something which looked like a gun and rushing out of the lecture hall in a hurry by a dusty leaf-colored jeep, and even though not quite sure, this informant had a vague recollection of the jeep's tag number."

"Objection, Your Honor," Lumumba jumped. "Are we going to indulge in hearsay and how much?"

"The witness is just getting started and you are jumping pre-maturely, Mr. Lumumba. Overruled! Continue Mr. Golden," the Judge ruled.

"There was another caller who also mentioned a bunch of people jumping into a dirty green colored jeep and trying to get away fast. Because of such corroboration, we immediately pulled up on the computer all jeeps registered with the Motor Vehicle Administration and narrowed our search on the MVA database to green colored jeeps. First, there weren't very many jeeps registered with the MVA, and whatever there were, green colored jeeps were only two in number. All State highway and street patrols were immediately alerted to look out for a green colored jeep. Two plain clothesed sheriffs in unmarked patrol cars were dispatched to the two registered jeep addresses for watchful observation and surveillance as we normally do in all cases suspected of hideout and criminal activity."

"And what feed back, if any, did you receive from any of your troops, Detective Golden?"

"No jeeps nor any residents were found at either of the addresses on the night of the shooting. However, at one of the addresses a jeep turned up the next day with three occupants coming out of the vehicle. One carried a gun and the other two opened the rear door and took out a deer, which seemed to be the prize of their hunt. Their gun registration and hunting license were checked and upon determining the *bona fide* of their gun possession activity, these folks were left alone by the deputies."

"What you are telling this Court seems to be all irrelevant, Detective Golden. What this Court needs to hear is the evidence you have in support of the charges against the Defendants," Judge Hamid interjected, imploring the Detective: "now, please get to the point."

"I have been answering the questions asked of me Your Honor! But now, I will ignore the detailed account and get to the point as you instructed. So after a painstaking follow up of all the gathered information and leads, a dirty green colored jeep was spotted on the other side of the hilly terrain near the river and a group of people living in a wooded area in a nearby ranch seemed to make use of it. All the activity going on in and around that area seemed mighty suspicious. Hence, authority was sought from the Magistrate for wire-tapping and installation of secret micro-listening and video recording devices for surveillance of the house and of the people coming in and out of there."

"Through the implanted listening devices, many conversations and discussions were recorded wherein the participants clearly held Dr. Watson as a Godless, anti-religious Frankenstein who needed to be 'wiped out' before it was too late and they made plans to accomplish this."

"After careful observation, surveillance, audio and video recordings of their conversations, boastful plans for ammunition gathering and assembly of home-made bombs, over a period of time sufficient probable cause was established to obtain a warrant for search, seizure and arrest of the defendants as suspects for conspiracy, aggravated assault and attempted murder of the victim as charged."

"That's not enough to hold these defendants under custody and they should be released on bail forthwith, Your Honor," demanded Lumumba.

"As Your Honor has pointed out, this is not a trial to prove the charges beyond a reasonable doubt. Rather, it is a preliminary hearing to merely establish whether there is enough evidence to bind the defendants to the grand jury, whose province it is to thoroughly examine all the evidence and determine whether or not to indict the defendants of the charged crimes. And, I submit, Your Honor, that for the purposes of this preliminary hearing, Detective Golden has amply presented justifiable bases for charging the defendants with the crimes, based on the evidence collected over a period of time by various means including audio and video recordings," asserted the States Attorney.

"Are there any further questions for Mr. Golden?" asked the Judge looking at the States Attorney.

"No, Your Honor," answered Philip Long.

"All right. You may now step down, Mr. Golden."

"Are there any other witnesses that the State wishes to present?

"No, Your Honor"

"Mr. Lumumba, does the defense wish to present any witness?"

"No, Your Honor!"

As a matter of tactics, the defense did not wish to reveal any of its strategies before the prosecution presented all the evidence. It was only then that the defense would consider if, at all, any rebuttal testimony were necessary. Until then the defense just wanted to wait and watch carefully the sum and substance of the State's case, making sure that the prosecution was procedurally within the bounds of the law.

"Based on the testimony presented, the Court is satisfied that there are sufficient grounds for suspecting the involvement of the defendants in the crimes charged and the defendants are, therefore, bound over to the grand jury. Until then the defendants shall remain in custody without bail," swiftly declared Judge Hamid, as many observers expected based on how this Judge usually ruled in such criminal cases.

Lumumba was flabbergasted at the Judge's decision because there was nothing of any substance or specificity, he reasoned, in the Detective's testimony, which in any way implicated the defendants with any particularity. Hence, there was no reason to deny bail to the defendants and keep them in custody. But Lumumba felt helpless. For there was little Lumumba could do to reverse the Judge's decision. He very well knew that as a trier of facts the Judge's findings would be hard to set aside and there wasn't much as a matter of law to challenge. That was the harsh reality Lumumba faced and he concluded that an appeal would be sheer waste of time, energy and resources without any realistic chance of a change in the outcome.

Lumumba was disgusted, but he briefly talked to the defendants before they were escorted out of the courtroom to the custody of the sheriff.

◆ 39 ◆

Even though grand juries are directed to independently examine and critically evaluate the evidence presented by the State in strict secrecy in the presence of only the defendant without the appearance of defense counsel, and had all the power to ask any questions to anyone and subpoena any person or documents, it was nevertheless a common notion among most observers of the system that grand juries usually did what the prosecutor wanted them to do. Indeed, some viewed the grand jury as nothing more than the "rubber stamp" of the prosecutor!

It's not how it's supposed to work, but its practicality that Lumumba had to reckon and deal with. And none to his surprise, the grand jury returned an indictment of the defendants on all three counts of conspiracy, aggravated assault and attempted murder.

The formalities of arraignment and pleading of "Not Guilty" as expected, took place per procedural requirements and the case was set for trial before Judge Hamid.

Using as much profiling, body-language and socio-psychological analyses as available and after exhaustive *voir dire* of a large pool of prospective jurors, the prosecutor and the defense counsel, taking full advantage of the privilege of peremptory strikes granted them, finally agreed on a panel of twelve jurors, ten males and two females. Both alternates were males.

During thorough *voir dire*, every prospective juror's views on the apparent conflict between scriptural faith and scientific system were elicited with particularity. But not a single juror was found who did not believe that it was blasphemous to denounce and assail God. That was the prevailing belief of the masses and regardless of whether or not the religious persuasion would have any effect on jury's verdict in this case, there wasn't much of a choice but to select the jury panel from within the population as it existed. The jury system was based, after all, on the premise that justice should be rendered by those who are peers of the accused.

The selected jury panel was, therefore, sworn and seated and the trial began.

Opening statements were presented with usual fervor by the State's Attorney, followed by the Defense Counsel, each pitching its contention; the prosecutor asserting that it will show beyond a reasonable doubt that the defendants were guilty as charged, and the defense counsel promising to prove that there was no merit to the State's case.

Warning the jury that the opening statements were only attorney's arguments and not evidence, Judge Hamid asked the State to call its first witness.

"State calls Deputy Elija Amir on the stand, Your Honor."

Elija Amir was sworn and seated.

"State your full name for the record."

"Elija Amir, Deputy Sheriff for Ocean County."

"Did you participate in investigating this case?"

"Yes, I did."

"Please tell the jury and the Court what you did and what you found."

"Having located the site where a dirty green colored jeep described by the informants was found, we had to determine whether the people associated with it were involved in any way with shooting and subsequent bombing death of Dr. Watson," began Elija Amir looking directly at the jury.

"And how did you make that determination?"

"The ranch from where the jeep was used appeared a focal gathering point of certain people. So we wanted to ascertain whether these folks were involved in the alleged criminal activity. The more we observed, followed and investigated the activities, the more we were convinced that this was a group of radical people with an extreme point of view and a missionary zeal for accomplishing their goal. They held a firm belief that it was the trend and influence of modern scientific thought and materialistic outlook that have taken men away from God and His Kingdom, with consequent moral decay, sexual perversions and erosion of family values. And it was the unchecked development of science and technology that has brought us to the point of tinkering with life itself, such as making assorted or cloned human embryos in petri dishes. This, the group held, was anti-life and Un-Godly even if it was all *in vitro* and the extracted stem cells saved and preserved life. And just as people fight and die to save their faith - Moslems against Jews, Protestants against Catholics and Communists against Capitalists - this group believed that it must likewise fight and eradicate atheistic science, thereby asserting 'God's Will'! So they targeted the champion of bioengineering, Dr. Watson, and vowed to blow him out of this universe! And this the defendants, Donald Hamilton and Robert Christian, accepted to faithfully carry out. And if they did not succeed in their attempt, a martyr volunteer was ready for the final act of wiping out the demon of Watson forever with his own life in suicide bombing. It was indeed an extreme fundamentalist group of devout believers."

"What evidence do you have, Deputy Amir, to prove what you just testified?" asked the prosecutor.

"Well, I have audio and video recordings made of multiple discussions, activities, conversations, exchanges and arguments between various members of the group, the defendants usually playing a leading role in group deliberations and planning. And, upon obtaining a warrant for search and seizure, when we entered and searched the ranch, we found several firearms including pistols, rifles, guns and bomb making instrumentalities. I would like to play those recordings before the court and one could then draw its own conclusions as to the culpability of these defendants," answered Deputy Amir.

"Such evidence is inadmissible, Your Honor," Lumumba quickly objected.

"Overruled," the Judge quickly snapped.

"I reserve my right to take exception, Your Honor," Lumumba shot back.

"Yes, you do. But go ahead Deputy Amir and play those recordings to the jury," the Judge ruled.

And the video recordings showed the following exchange between the police officer and Donald Hamilton:

The police officer: "Mr. Hamilton, you may choose to remain silent and seek legal counsel to answer any questions which may be used against you, or you may waive any such requirement and provide the information of your free will. What do you want to do?"

"I have nothing to hide, Officer. God is my Savior and He is always with me. What I really think, though, is that only those who are afraid of telling the truth go to attorneys and hide behind the technicalities to save their skin. And I have no intention of playing such a smart attorney game. So go ahead and ask me any question you like," responded

Hamilton.

"All right then, is it true that you and your colleagues belong to a group called the 'The Children of God'?"

"Yes, indeed."

"And, among other things, does this group believe that it is God who is Almighty; the omnipotent, omniscient and omnipresent? That, one should praise the Lord and abide by His wishes? That one goes to Hell if defiant of God?"

"Absolutely".

"And do you and the members of your group hold it Un-Godly that science rejects supra-natural providential force and recognizes only physical-chemical bases underlying all matter and creations, atomic or organic, animate or inanimate?"

"Yes, we do."

"And you also believe in defending and fighting for your belief, do you not?"

"I absolutely do."

"And didn't you think that Dr. Watson's research on human embryonic stem cells and other cloning experiments were anti-life and anti-God?"

"Yes, I did."

"And did the members of your group believe likewise?"

"Yes, they did."

"And doesn't your group also believe that if you

dedicate your life for a Holy cause and become a martyr, that you will be promised a place in Heaven?"

"That's correct."

"And when you and your group heard of Dr. Watson's forthcoming public presentation related to genomic-chemical basis of life and the possibilities related to "human cloning" at the celebrated Sunday Evening Forum, how did you and your group react, Mr. Hamilton?"

"Well, to tell the truth, we had several discussions and arguments among various members of our group and after thoughtful deliberations reached the conclusion that if people all over this world fight and die to save their faith and belief, we must also likewise fight science against God."

"And how did you and your group plan to accomplish that?"

"Very simple! One way or the other get rid of the crusader of cloning, Dr. Watson! If the leading voice and expert organizer of cloning research is silenced, that will be the first step in the right direction. We will then see what needs to be done next."

"Well, then plans must have been made to carry out the task. Isn't that right?"

"Of course! Me and my colleague Bob Christian volunteered to do the job and if it failed a martyr was ready to blow him out."

The jury listened and watched the recorded exchange with intense propensity. Some jurors even took notes.

Don Hamilton was an educated, perceptive and smart young man who also fervently believed in the teachings of the scriptures. From the very impressionable age of childhood, he was told that it is God who is the 'Creator'. That it is God who endowed men with soul and spirituality. That it is God who created Hell and Heaven. And it was a sin to revile God. As is most often the case, this is what Don Hamilton was given to understand and it was with this frame of mind Don Hamilton grew up. Little did he know that theology and philosophy were only as valid as the premise they were based on and that at the time these scriptures were written, the Earth was believed to be flat and stationary, the Sun was believed to be circling the Earth and neither the microscope, telescope, computer and DNA were known. But even if someone argued the validity of the principles of physics and biology, Don Hamilton couldn't forsake his mindset. Somehow the initial cerebral neural imprint in the brain seemed to form such an indelible impression on the mind that it appeared refractory to change.

Don Hamilton was deeply religious and believed in telling the truth. So he unhesitatingly answered all the questions asked of him.

And after the recordings were played, the prosecutor

had no further questions for Deputy Amir.

At this point the Judge struck his gavel declaring that the court will be in recess until 2 p.m.

40

Precisely at 2 p.m., the court reconvened and looking at the Defense Counsel the Judge said: "You may now cross-examine the Deputy," Mr. Lumumba.

Straightening out the necktie and buttons of his exquisite dark blue jacket Lumumba got up, walked toward the podium and positioned himself between the Deputy and the jury. His demeanor seemed to project a feeling that he was going to tear apart the Deputy's testimony.

Stepping forward and staring directly into the Deputy's eyes, Lumumba asked: "Deputy Amir, did you, at any time, personally see the defendants carry a gun?"

"No, sir."

"Do you know of anyone else who saw the defendants carry a gun and shoot Dr. Watson?"

"No, sir."

Thinking quick on his feet that the prosecution's chief witness has testified of no witness, no personal knowledge, or direct evidence of shooting, Lumumba figured that this is all he had to establish to win the case and to the surprise of everyone he abruptly declared: "No further questions, Your Honor."

Everyone seemed a bit astonished, as if taken aback! And there ensued a sudden stirred commotion throughout the courtroom. People turned their eyes toward each other as though clearly expressing disbelief and bewilderment at Lumumba's strange cross-examination.

The Judge immediately pounded his gavel and sternly said: "Order, Order! Please calm down, everyone."

Then turning to the Prosecutor, the Judge asked: "Any redirect, Mr. Long?"

"Yes, Your Honor," and so saying the Prosecutor turned toward the witness and asked: "Deputy Amir, do you know who made the recordings you just played before the court?"

"Yes, sir. I made the recordings while my assistant, Officer Mitch Miller, conducted interrogation of Mr. Hamilton."

"Has the recording been under your continuous custody all this time and are those recordings authentic, true and accurate in every respect as presented here to the court?"

"Yes, sir. The recordings have been under my uninterrupted custody all the time and it is authentic, true and accurate in every respect."

"No further questions, Your Honor."

"Mr. Lumumba, do you have any questions for the Deputy?" asked the Judge.

"No, Your Honor."

"Very well, you may now step down Deputy Amir," the Judge gestured.

"Any other witnesses, Mr. Long?" the Judge inquired.

"Yes, Your Honor. The State calls Officer Mitch Miller to the stand."

After the usual formality of the witness taking oath and stating its name and address, the Prosecutor began: "Mr. Miller, you saw the video recordings just played to the jury, did you not?"

"Yes, I did."

"As the recordings show, did you conduct the interrogation of Mr. Hamilton?"

"Yes, I did."

"And do you know who made the recordings just played before the court?"

"Yes, sir, my supervisor, Deputy Amir, made the recording while I conducted the interrogation."

"Are those recordings true and accurate in every respect as presented here to the Court?"

"Yes, they are absolutely true, correct and accurate."

"No further questions, Your Honor," said the Prosecutor concluding officer Miller's testimony.

"You may now cross-examine the witness Mr.

Lumumba," the Judge said looking at the Defense Counsel.

"No questions, Your Honor," quickly snapped Lumumba.

"All right, then. You may now step down, Mr. Miller," the Judge said while asking the Prosecutor: "any other witnesses, Mr. Long?"

"No, sir."

"Does the Defense wish to present any testimony?" the Judge asked Lumumba at this point, looking through his bifocal glasses.

"Yes, Your Honor. The Defense calls Mr. Robert Christian to the stand."

This was a bit bold and a surprising move on the part of the Defense Counsel, for he did not have to put the accused on the stand. It was a risky strategy seldom used by the Defense because being put on the witness stand the accused could not deny answering any question asked by the Prosecutor on cross-examination.

Called by the Defense Counsel, Robert Christian was seated in the witness chair and as usual he stated his name and address for the record, adjusting the microphone to proper angle.

No sooner did he finish taking the oath to tell the truth, whole truth and nothing but the truth than Lumumba asked: "Mr. Christian, did you carry a gun to the Sunday Evening Forum lecture of Dr. Watson and fired the shots?

"No, sir."

"Did you witness who did it?"

"No, sir."

"No further questions, Your Honor."

"You may now cross-examine the witness, Mr. Long," said the Judge.

Realizing that an elaborate questioning may complicate the issues, the Prosecutor strategically obviated any other inquiries and jumped at the only question that seemed to matter and asked in a deliberately casual manner in an ingenious attempt to extract an admission from the defendant: "Mr. Christian, you were present in the court and witnessed the video recordings of Donald Hamilton's interrogation, did you not?"

"Yes, I did."

"Isn't it true that after Donald Hamilton fired the shot at Dr. Watson with his telescopic silent rifle at the Sunday Forum, you and all your colleagues huddled and quickly escaped from the Forum in a green jeep?"

Even before Lumumba had a chance to raise an objection, the witness quickly answered: "No, not in a green but in a gray jeep."

"No further questions, Your Honor," the Prosecutor calculatingly, but very quickly, ended the questioning at this point and sat down, seemingly satisfied that his ploy of extracting an admission had succeeded.

It was a skillful strategy that worked, the Prosecutor thought. But he remained controlled in his professional composure without showing any sign of elated emotional reaction whatsoever while the whole court appeared spell bound with deadly silence. It all occurred in such a rapid sequence with abrupt end that no one even seemed to catch a breath.

Judge Hamid was equally surprised and Lumumba was out of his wits as to how it all began and suddenly ended in a manner that he neither expected nor contemplated!

The jury didn't seem perturbed as though it was all a matter of fact occurrence.

Judge Hamid, however, restored order and took control of the proceedings. Making eye contact with Mr. Lumumba through his bifocal, the Judge asked: "Any redirect for the witness, counselor?"

"No, Your Honor," Lumumba replied with seeming disgust and dejection.

"You may now step down, Mr. Christian," the Judge gestured while asking the Defense Counsel if he had any other witnesses?

"No, Your Honor," replied Mr. Lumumba.

"Are we ready for closing arguments, then," the Judge inquired.

Both attorneys nodded and Lumumba stepped forward to address the jury.

"Ladies and gentlemen of the jury," began Lumumba, "you have been presented not a shred of evidence by the State linking any of the defendants to any of the crimes with which they have been charged. It is noteworthy," Lumumba continued with an assertive voice, "that the State's main witness was Deputy Amir. And Deputy Amir admitted that he had no personal knowledge of defendants having fired the shots at Dr. Watson, nor did he know of any one else witnessing the shots having been fired by the defendants. And you must have noted, ladies and gentlemen of the jury, that the State presented no material or physical evidence at the trial linking or implicating the defendants of any of the crimes charged. In short, the State has failed to prove its case beyond a reasonable doubt and you must find the defendants 'not guilty' of the alleged crimes. Thank you, ladies and gentlemen of the jury," Lumumba concluded his brief but succinct argument and returned to his seat.

Lumumba thought that the more precise and to the point his arguments were, the more convincing and persuasive it might be for the jury to assimilate.

It was now the Prosecutor's turn to address the jury with its closing argument.

"Ladies and gentlemen of the jury," began Mr. Long with a subdued grin on his face, "did you notice how brief the defendant's closing argument was? That is so, because the defense had no argument," smiled Mr. Long as he moved from his seat to the podium facing the jury directly, leaving on his desk the yellow pad on which he had been taking copious notes during the trial. However, Mr. Long's associate, Sheela Verma, Assistant State's Attorney, was a thoughtful and astute observer keeping close track of the proceedings.

"Let me point out for the benefit of your deliberations," a tall and impressive Mr. Long continued in a clear authoritative voice, "it is well settled under the law of criminal conspiracy that an overt act of one partner in crime is attributable to all. Material support, allegiance to a particular common goal or agreement and collaboration of the group as a whole warrants each member as a causal agent of each act. Please note that it is less significant which of the member of a group committed the substantive offense than the fact that the crime was performed as part of a larger division of labor to which the defendant had also contributed his efforts. That is the law and that is how this case has to be adjudicated," asserted the Prosecutor. "Now the question is: 'Do the facts support the alleged criminal acts?' So remember, ladies and gentlemen, defendant Hamilton admitted to officer Miller that he was a member of a group called 'The Children of God' whose target was Dr Watson, the champion of bioengineering. And no one can put out of mind the avowed object of this group to 'blow him out of the universe'. And defendant Christian testified that after Donald Hamilton fired the shot at Dr. Watson with his telescopic silent rifle at the Sunday Forum, he and all his colleagues quickly escaped from the Forum in a jeep, albeit in a gray jeep. The exact identity of the color is not crucial, ladies and gentlemen! What is crucial is the fact that defendant Robert Christian admitted, perhaps unwittingly, nevertheless truthfully, to the firing of the shots. So now you know, ladies and gentlemen of the jury, that the basic elements of the offense of attempted murder and criminal conspiracy have been fully met by defendant's own testimony and you have no choice but to find the defendants guilty of the alleged crimes," concluded Mr. Long with an air of confidence typical of an experienced litigator, returning to his seat.

Judge Hamid then gave instructions to the jury, which was thereafter secluded for deliberations in a secured area. The Court then adjourned until further notice.

41

"Your presentation was flawless, both as to the law and the facts, Phil," Sheela commented as the State's Attorney and his team began to walk out of the courtroom pending jury deliberations. "There is no way we are going to lose conviction in this case, boss," Sheela further asserted, "unless..."

"Unless what?" Phil Long looked at Sheela with puzzled eyes.

"Unless," Sheela attempted to gather her energies before she wanted to say what was going through her mind, "unless, this conservative, God-abiding lay jury, feeling deeply about its beliefs, took the view that if the scientists insist on 'Playing God' by cloning a human or a human embryo, then the 'Believers' may likewise insist on 'blowing them out of this universe', and they could come out with a verdict of 'not guilty' without revealing their religious convictions by simply using the available technicality of State's failure to meet its burden of proof beyond a reasonable doubt."

"Do you really think the jury could do that?" Phil was incredulous of such a possibility.

"Why not, Phil? Their deliberations are held in strict secrecy and they don't have to disclose any part of it! As long as there is unanimity in their verdict and there is no coercion or malfeasance of any kind, the case is closed! Do I have to say more, Phil?" Sheela was forthright as she laid out the possibility, which Phil didn't contemplate.

"Juries are humans, too. They have their own faiths and beliefs. And, although they could be instructed to follow the law without bias or prejudice, it doesn't always happen that way, Phil. You know that, don't you?" Sheela added in an attempt to remind her boss.

"Yes, I am quite cognizant of human reactions, responses and realities, Sheela. But, thanks for the reminder." Phil Long was somber.

The whole broadcast media were abuzz with the incredible twists and turns of this unusual albeit short trial, involving some fundamental issues of immense public interest, of science and society, of law and beliefs, and of inherent limitations of democratic process to make critical policy decisions *vis-à-vis* new discoveries, knowledge and rapid technological advances occurring in all areas of natural sciences impacting society at large. And the commentators, legal scholars, religious authorities, ethicists and self-appointed *pundits* all had a field day with their opinions, theories and predictions on the outcome of the case. Or, rather what the outcome ought to be! It was interesting that no two commentators' views were congruent or similar and a decision of twelve laymen and women was going to be binding! That was the process and system of prevailing jurisprudence. The reality was that personal freedom, individuality and liberty were all contingent upon and confined within the norms and beliefs of a population wherein one happened to find itself in a given time and place. Defiance of prevalent norms was at one's own risk and peril of isolation and embarrassment. Some even wondered whether Professor Watson's demise wasn't simply a repeat of the inhuman history of humanity?

Lumumba took full advantage of every opportunity to appear on TV. That was how the bigshot attorneys gained fame and recognition, becoming rich in the process! But Mr. Long shunned media-hype and self-aggrandizement. He was a bit serious and the scholarly type, declining to make any comments while the case was pending. He was patient to wait for the jury verdict.

42

Late in the day, the Foreman of the jury informed the Judge that a verdict had been reached. The Judge immediately summoned the prosecutor, the defense counsel and the defendants, and the Court was scheduled to convene in 45 minutes. Somehow the news spread with lightening speed and the courtroom got fully packed with people anxious to hear the verdict.

Bringing order to the courtroom, Judge Hamid convened the session on time and sent for the jury to appear. There was pin drop silence in the courtroom as the jurors took their seat one by one. No overt expression of any kind was discernible on the jury faces. After determining that everything was in order, the Judge asked: "Mr. Foreman of the jury, has the jury reached a verdict?"

"Yes, Your Honor," and the Foreman handed the verdict to the Bailiff who presented it to the Judge.

After examining the verdict, the Judge returned it to the Foreman and asked the Foreman to read the verdict.

"On each count of conspiracy, aggravated assault and attempted murder, the jury finds the defendants **'Not Guilty'.**"

There was an immediate commotion all over the courtroom. Some faces looked surprised, some bewildered and some had a happy grin. Mixed reaction was apparent and people started mulling around in the courtroom with their own interpretation of the verdict.

"Order! Order!" Judge Hamid struck the gavel several times and soon everyone quieted down.

The jury was polled individually as to the verdict and all formalities having been satisfied, the Judge thanked the jury, the legal counsels and adjourned the proceedings.

Whether guilty or not guilty, the news media had pre-programmed a special report in anticipation of the jury verdict. It was a story like this that the news media relished for higher ratings. No matter what the outcome, they always had spin-doctors and eager commentators who loved to talk, proffer opinions and be seen on the 'tube'.

Lily and Samir were following the proceedings with interest and the verdict did not come to them as any surprise.

The University faculty found it painfully disappointing how the legal system worked. The lawmakers were mostly lawyers and together with the bar associations they pretty much watched every legislative move that could affect their pecuniary interest, notwithstanding the criticism that they had succeeded in converting the legal process into a most litigious system. The plaintiffs' attorneys thrived on filing suits even on contingencies, if they saw big bucks coming in. Retaining about one-third of settlement or award wasn't a bad bargain.

It was intriguing that while the judicial system was structured to ascertain and uphold the truth, the murderer, the rapist and the criminal were peculiarly protected from confession for fear of self-incrimination. It was left to the prosecutor to establish the truth. And even if the offender admitted to its legal counsel of having committed the crime and provided full details of when, where and how the crime was committed, the attorney was mandated never to disclose any of it and keep it wrapped up in secrecy under a fascinating attorney-client privilege. If the attorney felt uncomfortable, all he could do was to decline representation, but he could never disclose anything said to him in confidence by the client. Even more interesting was the role the hired defender had to play in zealously defending the criminal; that is, to set him free of any criminal charges. That's what he was paid for!

It was left to the State to establish the criminality and not just prove, but prove beyond a reasonable doubt the guilt of the suspect. And it was for the art and clever tricks, for the ability to find holes in the State's case, and for knowing how, when and what legal tactics and technicalities to employ that the criminal defense lawyers were recognized and famous for. And it was 'Big Bucks' that bought them! Show the money and you can have them! You have no luck in saving your skin if you don't have the dough! Whatever the intent of the system, it appeared as though what really mattered was 'Big Bucks', so that the hired cracker jack, high-fly zealous defender could somehow defeat the State from establishing the charges, thereby exculpating the suspect of any criminality. For the system provided that one was innocent until proven guilty.

It was a captivating trial and the public watched the drama and the thrill of the story being told all over in the news media, which were good at creating suspense and sensation!

43

The newly elected parliament was scheduled to convene on the first Monday of autumn.

As the members assembled in the great 'Hall of Freedom' at the center of the elegant, pink marbled, circular domed, lavishly furnished parliament building, a great applause greeted Lily as she entered the magnificent hall. Her unconventional and courageous conduct of an election campaign based on a principled stand and miraculous escape from suicide bombing were a matter of great satisfaction and pride for the fellow members and she was joyfully hugged and kissed by those who were close to her. She was humbled by the depth of appreciation and affection bestowed upon her.

True to her campaign promise, however, the first order of business for Lily during this parliament session was to introduce a bill to ban public sale, use and possession of firearms and assault weapons. And, so she did.

As was typical of politicians, there was impassioned debate opposing the bill by those beholden to the gun-lobby, which had pulled all stops to defeat the bill.

Lily was different in her approach to politics. She was firmly of the view that the best politics was to be true to your people and principles. There may be temporary setbacks and loss of gained position and power, she realized, but it was precisely such sacrifice, the sincerity of purpose and the tested honesty and integrity of one's character that endured. People couldn't be fooled all the time and they readily came to recognize the opportunists despite all the publicity, rhetoric, fanfare and spins. Lily was confident and self-assured. Therefore, in her preface to the introduction of the bill, Lily let it be understood that should the bill fail, she will resign from the parliament and launch a vigorous campaign to recall all those who voted against the bill.

There was immense stir in the parliament as Lily made those remarks. Everyone knew that Lily was serious and she meant every word of what she said. She had proven to be a person of steadfast inner conviction and strength, a force to be reckoned with. However, the pragmatic politicians were shrewd enough to calculate that her declared commitment was too idealistic to be practical in a democratic parliamentary setup where the art and operative words were "negotiation" and "compromise."

While the parliament continued debating the issue at length, the savvy firearm industry lobbyists tried behind the scene to convince the members with huge campaign fund donations that the odds of recall were really slim and if she resigned, as she said she would, the leading voice and the issue would disappear from the parliament and the ban would never occur! It should be obvious, the lobbyists argued, that the most expedient strategy, therefore, should be the defeat of the bill at the first instance and worry about the rest later. What better opportunity to kill the bird in its own nest without throwing a stone, the lobbyists were gleeful at pointing out.

Preservation of position and power were paramount to

the members and they needed all the money they could get to campaign in this age of hard core manipulative advertisement and media-influenced elections. In addition to the lobbyists' pitch, sheer reality and self-interest were reasons enough for some shrewd members to cast their vote against the bill despite overt statements to the contrary. And the bill was defeated.

Lily resigned.

44

Lily's resignation came as a shocking blow to her constituents and the media interrupted regular programming to carry the news. Even though she did not ask, this time every TV channel sought her appearance on prime time. While Lily went in calm consultation with her supporters assembled on short notice at the University Forum to plan an appropriate strategy, Samir took charge of handling the media and scheduling her appointment with as many reporters as possible. Local, national and global broadcasters had hurriedly swarmed all round the Forum doorstep amid buzzing sensation of this unusual event.

An assemblage of microphones from various news agencies quickly got set up at the bottom of the steps in front of the Forum hall and cameramen were waiting for Lily to come out and make a statement.

As Lily stepped out after a strategy session with her supporters, an immediate hustle-bustle ensued amid the broadcast crew and one reporter suddenly yelled: "Why did you resign, Ma'am?"

By then Lily had arrived in front of the microphones and she quickly remarked: "Although rhetoric, double-talk and hypocrisy are not uncommon in politics, isn't that one of the reasons why people have become increasingly cynical, losing faith in the prevailing system? And isn't it worrisome that the system has been so politicized that about half the voting population doesn't even care to exercise its right of franchise?" Lily was forthright as she unhesitatingly expressed her views to the crowd.

"No doubt I could have continued despite defeat of the bill, but it would have been utterly unconscionable to consider myself a worthy representative of the people, if the purpose for which I was elected couldn't be accomplished. Politics ought to be more than preserving one's power and position," Lily was frank.

"And now being outside, how are you going to help the cause?" a reporter asked.

"Well, people have the right to recall those who betrayed their trust. However, if we just sit silent and let it all go idly by, which is what these seasoned politicians are counting on, nothing will change. And things will go on like they always have. Someone has to take the lead with bold initiative and organize the recall. There has to be a consequence to their action and we must make them realize it," Lily was emphatic.

"And how do you propose to accomplish that?" inquired another loud voice.

"I am quite cognizant that there is inherent inertia in the masses and it takes special organization, dedication and leadership to convince the people and overcome public scepticism and apathy. I also know that unshakable perseverance and sacrifice are required to generate a sustainable public movement of undeniable impact. Nevertheless, I am determined to devote all my energies to make it happen," Lily declared.

Her comments were televised by all news media on prime time and repeated several times on later newscasts.

It was amazing that as soon as Lily's comments flashed over the wires, her headquarters got inundated with phone calls extolling her decision with resolute support for her courageous stand. Peoples' response was phenomenal!

Lily felt elated, convinced and confident. She was prepared for the challenge.

Samir was more resolved to bringing about a change in the system.

45

It appeared as though people loved the challenge and craved for action, particularly the younger folks. Lily didn't lose any time and immediately began a massive drive to collect signatures for a petition to recall those members of parliament who had reversed their manifest position and voted against "Ban the Gun" bill.

It was a narrow margin of merely two votes by which the bill was defeated. So, Lily calculated that even if the recall of only one member succeeded, no one would ever dare to oppose the legislation when it came back for re-vote. More importantly, Lily wanted the recall to demonstrate and establish the superior and supreme power of people over politics and parliament.

The stakes were high and Lily was determined not to leave any stone unturned. Therefore, day after day, despite all the difficulties, Lily would go from ward to ward and precinct to precinct, wherever invited, to be with people who just so much wanted to meet this maverick figure of charismatic character and uncommon ways.

While Lily mingled with folks gathered at school halls, churches, civic centers, play grounds or other common assembly places, Samir would stand by her side holding a big poster prominently displaying: "NOT THE POLITI-

CIANS', BUT PEOPLES' POWER SHALL PREVAIL."

They loved the slogan and were anxious to participate in this movement of 'first impression.' They couldn't wait to sign the petition, several sheets of which Samir made sure to have spread on a large table by his side so that everyone could get to sign it without forming long lines.

Lily loved people and people loved Lily. Perhaps it was her simple, forthright and unassuming openness that touched them and at every gathering she was warmly cheered and complimented for taking up the cause and sticking with it.

Seeing Samir standing by her side with the poster, some would occasionally remark: "Isn't it wonderful that you have a husband who is so supportive and dedicated?" to which Lily simply responded by moving over a little and wrapping Samir with her arms, her tearful expressive eyes saying it all.

Samir just smiled and held her close while spontaneous applause of affectionate appreciation admired this extraordinary couple.

46

While the recall campaign was in full swing, Lily developed a low-grade fever accompanied by extreme fatigue. She had also lost some weight and looked a little pale. Samir got worried but Lily explained it away as merely something probably resulting from exhaustion due to strenuous campaigning. Taking it easy and resting a bit ought to resolve it; she tried to console Samir.

"Give me a couple of Tylenol and a glass of cold water. I shall lie down for awhile and I think I will be all right," Lily made an effort to comfort Samir and allay his worry.

Samir felt troubled, nevertheless. Lest Lily notice it, Samir tried to keep his anxiety hidden without saying much to Lily, sitting quietly by her bedside with the palm of his hand on Lily's forehead asking her to close the eyes and relax.

Holding Samir's hand, Lily soon dozed off.

Samir felt a little relieved.

So that Lily would have something appetizing to eat when she woke up, Samir went into the kitchen to fix up a dish that would entice Lily. But when Lily got up from the nap, she didn't have any appetite.

Samir's worry deepened and he decided to make an appointment with their family physician, Dr. Piya Nilu. Even though it was late in the afternoon, he called Dr. Nilu and discussed Lily's complaints. Dr. Nilu understood Samir's concern and despite her schedule being full, made an appointment to see Lily first thing the next morning. Meanwhile Dr. Nilu suggested having some stat blood tests done before she saw Lily the next day. Although Dr. Nilu's office wasn't very far, in light of Lily's indisposition Dr. Nilu arranged the nurse in her office to go to Lily and draw the blood for stat lab work.

The next morning Dr. Nilu examined Lily in her office. A thorough physical exam together with the results of the blood tests seemed to have raised enough concerns in Dr. Nilu's mind that she wanted Lily to be admitted to the hospital for further tests. She indicated to Lily and Samir that she wasn't sure exactly what was going on and it was prudent to conduct further tests to rule out certain possibilities and arrive at a definitive diagnosis.

At the University hospital Lily was almost a celebrity. Although the staff considered it a pleasure and privilege to attend to Lily, nevertheless the mere fact that she was being admitted to the hospital raised some worrisome anxiety in everyone's mind.

Dr. Nilu ordered a thorough work up and it was all carried out expeditiously.

Piya Nilu was an outstanding internist, well recognized and respected for her clinical abilities. Yet, she was unable to pin point Lily's condition to any specific cause despite the results of blood chemistry, CBC and radiological screening. Although the tests revealed some abnormal results and Lily was getting more jaundiced with progressive enlargement of the liver, Dr. Nilu wasn't able to reach a definitive diagnosis, albeit she had formed some notion in her mind which she thought was ominous enough not to discuss prematurely with either Lily or Samir.

Meanwhile Lily's fever was spiking.

Dr. Nilu did not think it wise to start any therapy without clinching the diagnosis, other than to treat Lily symptomatically. In light of Lily's worsening condition, however, she decided to perform a bone marrow biopsy so as to confirm what she thought might be the malady.

After two independent readings of the biopsy slides, Pathology reported a diagnosis of non-Hodgkin's lymphoma, confirming Piya Nilu's worst fears.

Particularly because she knew Samir so well, Dr. Nilu felt deeply saddened. But she did not overtly express any feeling while discussing the diagnosis with Samir and Lily, explaining all the therapeutic options available and lymphoma's positive response to chemotherapy, which had to be started immediately.

Surprisingly, Lily wasn't upset or disheartened. Rather, she was self-assured to win over this cancer. And she said to Samir while looking at Piya Nilu: "Don't you worry. I am not going to leave you Samir. I just can't, no matter what," and so saying she hugged Samir, tears rolling down over both of their faces.

Dr. Nilu headed straight to Oncology to discuss Lily's diagnosis and arrange for chemotherapy with the Department's specialist on lymphomas.

The news of Lily's diagnosis sent shock waves throughout the campaign headquarters and news bulletins started flashing all over the broadcast media.

Even though a bit indisposed, Lily had great strength of willpower and she accepted celebrated TV anchor Larry Kingle's request for an interview, which Larry arranged at the hospital conference room.

People appeared anxious to see and hear their beloved Lily for whom they seemed to have developed a special bond, particularly in light of her diagnosis.

It is peculiar that adversity often brings people closer together!

To Larry's first question inquiring as to the prospective status of the recall campaign in light of her diagnosis, Lily replied: "This campaign is not related to whether Lily lives or dies, Larry. What is at stake here is the demonstration of peoples' power over machinations and betrayal of the politicians. And I urge all my fellow citizens not to get disheartened over my condition but to pledge all out support for the recall, thereby firmly asserting fundamental principles of an electoral democratic system. As far as I am concerned, I can't wait to be back on the campaign trail as soon as my therapy is over."

"How are you feeling at the moment, though?" Larry gently inquired.

"Other than feeling a little fatigued, I am doing fine.

The lymphoma has been caught at a very early stage and the development of molecularly-designed targeted chemotherapy tailored on the basis of my individual genetic profile should help alleviate the problem. Pharmacogenomics and drug design based on receptor analyses have advanced so far that only the malignant cells are targeted without affecting normal cellular functions. Consequently, the patient does not get immuno-compromised, a landmark achievement in modern chemotherapy. Besides, there are minimal side effects. However, relapse could still be a possibility and as you know, Larry, recurrence of lymphoma would be the bearer of 'Bad News'!"

"Precisely for that reason, has cloned embryonic stem cell transplant been considered? I should think that you have been apprised of this new life-saving therapeutic modality, particularly in light of this University's Laboratory of Bioengineering being the pioneer in this revolutionary technology," Larry inquired.

"As you mentioned, Larry, it is remarkable and fortunate for me that scientists have succeeded in directing human embryonic stem cells to produce hematopoietic cells that can generate all components of blood including platelets, red and white cells. And the major problem of immune rejection is overcome by autologous cloned embryonic stem cells so that when these cloned embryonic hematopoietic stem cells are grafted into bone marrow after chemotherapy, a complete rejuvenation is achieved, wiping out malignancy."

"Some object to extracting human embryonic stem cells on moral and ethical grounds, tantamount to destruction of *potential* human life. Obviously, you have no such qualms," Larry interjected.

"It is quite interesting that you bring up this moral and ethical question. Let's think for a moment about this much argued issue of '*potential*' human life. A sugar, a phosphate and a four-unit base together have the *potential* of becoming DNA only if proper and sufficient conditions exist. And a chain of DNA has the *potential* of forming a living organism only if proper and sufficient conditions occur. And a human sperm has the *potential* of forming a human only if it conjugates with a human egg and the resulting fertilized egg gets implanted into a human uterus. So you see Larry, *potential* in itself has no consequence until proper, requisite and sufficient conditions prevail. Therefore, putting an isolated human egg and sperm together in a petri dish for fertilization and allowing the fertilized egg to grow to a certain stage *in vitro,* shall never have the *potential* of any life until proper and sufficient conditions are obtained in a human womb. Thus, as I have repeated Larry, every atom and molecule, hence all matter has the *potential* of becoming a life, provided proper and sufficient conditions occur. Therefore, destruction of matter would be a destruction of *potential* life! Clearly, this notion of *potentiality* assumes an aura of absurdity if taken to its ultimate logical end. Certainly, no one would subscribe to such an extreme position. The question then becomes how and where a line is to be drawn? Who defines what 'Life' is? What is the fundamental attribute that distinguishes 'living' and 'animate' from 'non-living' and 'inanimate'? The answer may seem obvious and simple but even biologists specializing in ontology have difficulty in arriving at a defining demarcation at the fundamental level. Come to think of it, Larry, it all may be "*conditional*" rather than 'absolute'!

"In short, all I want to point out is that extraction of stem cells from a defined cluster of a cloned embryo or a fertilized egg grown in a synthetic medium in a petri dish is not a destruction of *life*, potential, real or otherwise. It ought to be self-evident, Larry, that a bunch of cells floating in a petri dish cannot be equated with 'life' anymore than a bunch of unsculptured marble pieces can be equated with Tullio Lombardo's '*ADAM*' ! In other words, what needs to be understood, Larry, is that all cells, embryonic or non-embryonic, somatic or gametic, have the *potential* of whatever we want to make of them, even a cloned human, only if given proper and sufficient conditions to make it happen. The secret and success lie in unraveling and controlling the self-regulatory mechanisms of gene action, interaction and expression on a progressive temporal continuum. With advances in science and technology, it's now not a matter of *whether*, but of *when* and *how*."

"I see your point, Lily. But I am not sure that the religious, moralists and ethicists would agree."

"Well, Larry, whether they agree or not, we can't avoid facing the facts and reality. It should be quite obvious that the values of morals and ethics are dependent on time, place and the stage of societal evolution, sophistication and epistemological advancement. What may be moral and ethical under one set of conditions may not be moral and ethical in another. Harem and slavery were in vogue at one time, but immoral, unethical and illegal now. Having sex before getting married was abhorrent and immoral at one time, but living together is now nothing to talk about. Gay or lesbian relationships and rights were unthinkable not very long ago, but now legal recognition is not uncommon to find."

"Apart from a continuum of changing legal, ethical and moral standards, attitudes and values, isn't it strange, Larry, that a State in the name of sovereign power granted to it by its people, doesn't find it immoral or unethical to destroy a human life by death sentence, but finds it immoral and unethical to extract a bunch of cells from an embryonic cluster grown in a petri dish? Indeed, the stem cells are isolated to save human lives, not to destroy them. Of course, dichotomies and disparities are nothing new in human thought and history, Larry, but scientists must proceed with their work objectively. That is how science has progressed and that is how it is going to move forward. There certainly would be rejection, repression, denunciation, disapproval, opposition, sanctions, suffering and reprisals along the way, but we only have to remember the fate self-acclaimed righteous men befell on Galileo, Socrates and Bruno," Lily was forthright.

"Scientific objectivity is not easily accepted or perceived even by intelligentsia, let alone by common folks, I admit. And it is only a truism that progress doesn't follow an easy or smooth straight path. Somehow humans seem to have inherent inertia against change! And some folks denounce cloning experiments in any form, whether 'therapeutic' or 'reproductive,' arguing that it degrades 'human life and dignity'," Larry interjected.

"This is nothing new, Larry. The moralists and ethicists raised the same kind of fuss when *in vitro* fertilization began and the first test tube baby was born. And they talked of "Playing God" when the first human heart transplant took place. I suppose this is how they justify their existence! Nevertheless, it should be quite instructive, Larry, to determine from these folks, who so loftily extol the value and virtue of 'human life and dignity,' where their concern, compassion and sense of moral outrage are when before their very eyes scores of children die of hunger all over this Earth and homeless humans cry for minimal 'life and dignity,' while these benevolent protectors of human conscience innocently look the other way and enjoy a comfortable life playing big-time leadership roles! It is strange and ironic, Larry, that not unusually, this is the sad reality of human behavior and social dynamics!"

"I understand what you mean. But, be it as it may, the plan of your medical team appears to be proceeding with a hematopoietic cloned stem cell bone marrow transplant following chemotherapy. Is that correct, Lily?" Larry tried to ascertain.

"Yes. They are going to implant the nucleus from one of my somatic cells into an enucleated egg and then stimulate the egg to resume its normal function of cell division and growth toward forming an embryonic cluster wherefrom the stem cells could be derived. These embryonic stem cells shall then be induced to transform into blood-forming hematopoietic cells for bone marrow transplant. Since these hematopoietic cells will be genetically identical, a stable graft without any immune rejection shall occur and I should be free of cancer. That is the plan, that is the strategy, and that is the hope, Larry."

"We wish you every success and a full recovery, Lily."

So saying Larry concluded the interview without prolonging it any further.

Lily was getting a little tired and she whispered with a sweet smile: "So long, Larry."

47

The live interview with Larry was watched on TV with much curiosity by everyone eager to see and hear Lily after learning of her infliction with cancer in the midst of the recall campaign. Her open, forthright, frank and factual answers must have touched such a responsive cord that the hospital had to make special arrangements to receive the overwhelming number of flowers, get-well-cards and letters that started pouring in.

Samir would read them all to Lily and both of them would sometimes cry over the love and affection wrapped in those simple words that could have emanated only from the universality of human sensitivity. It was inexplicable how human feelings transcended all boundaries of logic, reason or relationships. It was mere semantics whether those expressions were called 'sympathies,' 'well wishes' or 'prayers.' Nevertheless, they were very comforting and heartwarming for Lily. It made her feel that she was not alone in her struggle, that the whole world was by her side. Even though amorphous, wasn't this the essence of humanity? Lily pondered and asked Samir to carefully save those cards and letters. She wanted to read them again in a quiet moment when she returned home and write a personal note to as many as she could. It was all very sentimental and it seemed quite apparent that emotion had a deeper domain and dimension, distinct from the realm of reason and reality.

Knowing that lymphoma could be deadly, Samir felt devastated despite the promise of a stem cell transplant. More painful were Lily's words that "*I am not going to leave you, Samir. I just can't*," which constantly swirled in his mind, particularly when Lily would be sleeping in an inclined position on the hospital bed and he would be sitting by the bedside staring at the I.V. fluid dripping drop by drop into her vein. Anxiety would suddenly grip him but he was confident of the medical miracles, which kept his hopes alive.

Having accepted the faculty position at the University, Samir had to teach two courses during the current semester, Astronomy 101 and Astrophysics 301. The Department was well aware of Lily's hospitalization and apart from the teaching load and occasional faculty meetings or attendance to routine matters, the Department was graciously supportive of Samir being away at the hospital with Lily. Being within the same campus, it became easier for Samir to walk back and forth from the Department to the hospital within minutes.

At the Oncology wing, every patient had a private room

and at Samir's request a folding cot was provided so that he could stay overnight close to Lily, for it was unbearable for him to see her lying alone in a hospital bed and not have her within his eyesight. Lily tried to persuade Samir that because chemo couldn't be given at home, she had to be at the hospital. And the nurses and the staff were all so caring that there was no need for him to stay overnight and not get proper rest at home. Samir listened carefully and at the end, bending over a little and kissing her gently, simply whispered: "You are so naive, my love! You just don't understand! I cannot explain but I am going to be right here by your side."

Lily didn't say a word more and, whether it was her sensitivity or weakness, tears simply rolled down from her happily closed eyes.

Except for those hours, which were fixed by his teaching schedule, Samir would spend all his time with Lily and feed her with his own hands whenever there was an opportunity to do so. Lily could see that somehow it made Samir happy and she never resisted. Indeed, it reminded her of similar earlier times with Samir, which made her feel very happy as well.

Even though Lily had resigned, the volunteers at her parliamentary headquarters had vowed to carry on the recall campaign, particularly in light of her being indisposed and admitted to the hospital. So that the impetus of the recall campaign remained at its heightened tempo, once during the week and once at the weekend, Samir would devote about 2.5 hours in the evening, after feeding supper to Lily, to meet the folks gathered at a precinct venue pre-arranged by the campaign volunteers. At every meeting an enlarged photograph of Lily, prominently mounted on a big poster, was set by the table where the recall petition was kept for signatures.

After a jovial introduction of Samir by the campaign volunteers as "*Lily's husband and professor of astronomy*" Samir would make brief informal remarks about Lily's treatment and progress at the hospital, and then he would move around in the gathering trying to greet everyone. Curiously, people were excited and delighted to talk to this unassuming professor of astronomy who was so much at ease in telling them in simple terms the mysteries of galaxies, black holes, 'event horizon' and such other topics. They were just charmed and fascinated by the eloquence of discourse that Samir so effortlessly engaged these folks in grasping the dynamic workings of the cosmos. After expressing their heart-felt well wishes for Lily, they signed the recall petition and Samir then returned to the hospital.

Lily anxiously waited to hear the details of every meeting and she felt a big surge of joy and energy knowing how well Samir had supplanted the campaign, which was progressing so successfully.

Lily felt elated and full of hope, which seemed so necessary to nurture her body and soul at these difficult times. Neuroendocrine interactions concomitant to stress alleviation were reported by psychosomatic studies to influence the disease as well as the healing and recovery process through humoral, immunological and physiological mediation. Notwithstanding such studies, Lily was always calm, cheerful and positive in her thinking. Her self-confidence and optimism also helped Samir to allay subconscious fear and anxiety that her diagnosis had created within him. Every diversion from constant thinking of Lily's condition was perhaps conducive to Samir's well being as well, and going to these gatherings and talking to assembled folks was good for Samir's psyche. Peoples' response, consolation and support were very uplifting for Samir and he returned with renewed vitality after every meeting. Samir's enthusiastic narration of the details of these meetings filled Lily with great excitement and she couldn't wait to be back on the campaign trail as soon as the therapy was complete.

Genomically tailored and molecularly targeted chemotherapy went very well without undue nausea, loss of hair or other awful side effects and the tests indicated that Lily was in complete remission. Preparations were, therefore, under way for the cloned stem cell transplant and Lily was allowed to go home and recuperate until then.

Lily was happy being back at home.

Although she may have now appeared to look a little thin (something most women so much wanted to achieve in this fashionable modern world), Samir teased her that she actually looked prettier than before and some of the fancy intimate garments he had picked at the Kashmir open market may now fit her better! As was her nature, Lily felt a little shy at Samir's remarks but quipped: "You mean, I should try them on? Right?"

"I didn't say that. All I stated was a factual observation. You can interpret it any way you want."

"All right then, I disagree."

"But, what if I insist?"

"Then, I don't know."

"Yes, you do," and so saying Samir gently pulled Lily close, to which she didn't resist. Samir made her feel like a newlywed bride all over again and Lily reciprocated fully.

Samir was overjoyed having Lily back home and he surprised Lily with a gourmet dinner that he prepared using all the culinary art he had developed while being at the University away from home. If there was one temptation to which Samir easily succumbed, it was the taste of delicious food of all delectable delicacies.

Just the sight and aroma of prepared dishes made Lily hungry and she didn't hesitate to take full advantage of the manner and ambiance of service that only her devoted husband could render with such loving care.

Samir sat adoringly next to Lily and he was ecstatic watching Lily's appetite return to normal. It was a very happy moment for him.

Lily was overjoyed being home and as she was preparing to head toward the bedroom to change for the night, Samir handed her a closed envelope and asked Lily to open it only when she was ready to retire.

Lily knew the soft, sweet and romantically imaginative side of intellectual Samir and this secretive envelope made her all the more curious and anticipative. So she quickly changed into an attractive intimate nightgown and slipped into bed, for she couldn't wait to open the envelope. And what she found was a letter, which said as follows:

WELCOME HOME MY LOVE!

Though the dawn broke the shadow of the night,
And the buds opened their heart to sunny delight,
Though the birds sang sweet melody,
And the bees kissed for nectar,
Though the warm wind was soothing,
But without you, My Love,
This home was Nothing!

Perhaps you wouldn't know,
Life without you is a void, My Lil,
I do not know how to say,
But it is only YOU that can fill.

Welcome Home My Love!

Reading Samir's letter,
Lily couldn't help but cry,
Tears kept rolling over her rosy cheeks,
Until they got dry!

48

Over the weekend, Samir was scheduled for another public meeting arranged by the campaign staff. Being at home, Lily called the campaign office to get an update and was told that the number of signatures had far exceeded the required total. But, because people were still enthusiastic and calling to sign the petition, they thought it was a good idea to continue holding the meetings and keep peoples' interest and spirits up.

Apart from Samir's elucidative discussion of the significance of the recall campaign in a parliamentary democracy, the staff reported that people were extremely delighted by his artful co-mingling of the political with the esoteric of astronomy in such simple terms and ease that they enjoyed listening to the relationship of the laws of physics and cosmic phenomena with awe and fascination. He made people think of these meetings more as fun and not mere politics. "He is so natural," they would say coming out of the meeting.

Not so surprisingly, Samir equally well enjoyed these 'get togethers.'

Prior to going to a scheduled meeting, Samir thought that it might be good for Lily to get out and surprise everyone by her unanticipated appearance at the meeting. But on second thought he decided against it for fear that it may be too exhausting. He anticipated that everyone would then want to come, touch and talk to Lily to express heart-felt happiness at her recovery and good health. Mere common courtesy would dictate this to be unavoidable. Resulting undue excitement and demand on her energies during recuperation while the stem cell transplant was still to take place didn't seem such a smart idea. Hence, Samir didn't even suggest it to Lily.

Having learned from the campaign staff of people's continuing demand for Samir and knowing how logical and articulate Samir was, Lily was happy that "*Lily's husband and professor of astronomy*" was a big hit. But, even if subconsciously, the fear lingered in her mind that despite all the breakthroughs in modern medicine brought about by the new frontiers of biotechnology and human genomics, there still could be a chance for lymphoma to take a toll on her life. Should this happen, Lily found solace in the thought that Samir could keep the campaign alive!

Human potential is often revealed through the demand of circumstances, Lily realized as Samir carried on the recall campaign. She felt very proud of him.

Now that the statutory requirements for the recall petition were fully met and Lily was in complete remission, Samir thought that it might be opportune to submit the petition prior to Lily undergoing cloned stem cell transplant.

Agreeing wholeheartedly, Lily didn't hesitate to reveal her mind, telling Samir: "Life is unpredictable, Samir. Therefore, let's accomplish all we can while I have regained health. But this ought to be a well arranged public event, don't you think?"

"Of course, Lil," Samir responded and took charge again, calling TV anchor Larry Kingle.

Larry was thrilled to hear of Lily's recovery and wanted to fully cover the submission of the recall petition to the Speaker of Parliament. Samir informed Larry that the petition will be submitted in the middle of the week on Wednesday afternoon at 4 O'clock, and that all citizens were invited to assemble at the Parliament House. A huge turnout was expected, both to felicitate Lily for her recovery and to demonstrate their strength and solidarity for the cause. People wanted the Parliament to take notice of public determination and resolve. They expected the parliament to act decisively.

The word that after chemotherapy Lily was in complete remission and that she will submit the recall petition on

Wednesday at 4 p.m., spread rampant through every news channel and there was a fresh excitement among the citizenry to attend and participate in this momentous event.

49

Beginning around 3:30 p.m., the crowd began to thicken and by the time it was 4 p.m., the entire ground in front of the Parliament was fully packed with people. It was an unprecedented assembly of citizens at the parliament and the outpouring of such solidarity and resolute support overwhelmed Lily.

Aware of prior violent demonstrations and incidences, the police were at full alert and security around the Parliament House was tightened. The Speaker of Parliament was kept fully informed of all developments.

Being an elected representative of the people and sensitive to public sentiments and opinion, the Speaker thought it sensible to come out of the Chamber and greet the people assembled outside and personally receive the 'Recall Petition'.

Politicians savor public adoration and the Speaker wanted to make the most of this unique opportunity to show the people his sensitivity, receptivity and recognition of their cause.

Expecting that the people would like to hear a few words from Lily and the Speaker, the campaign workers had brought with them a hand-held megaphone, which the security police readily cleared. As the Speaker came down to the foot of the steps of the Parliament House, Lily warmly greeted him while the people applauded cheerfully.

Lily then took the megaphone and said: "Mr. Speaker! On behalf of the citizens of this parliamentary constituency, I am honored to present to you this Petition to recall certain members of the parliament whom the electorate deems to be unworthy of their representation. The Petition asks the parliament to act promptly and decisively. We thank you for coming out, meeting us and accepting the Petition."

With those remarks, Lily handed over the Petition to the Speaker and the crowd applauded with triumphant enthusiasm.

The Speaker then took the megaphone in his hand and addressing the people, remarked: "My fellow citizens! This is a great day for our democratic process. Through this Recall Petition you have demonstrated one more time that with resolute determination, peoples' persevered struggle can change any system, authority or rule no matter how autocratic, resistant, repressive, powerful or dismissive of peoples' will it may be. The recall petition proves that ultimately it is the peoples' power that prevails. I commend Lily's courage, conscience and commitment to the highest principles of electoral democracy and assure you that the Parliament will act on the petition decisively and discharge its duty faithfully under the Constitution. It is equally significant that this has been an orderly and peaceful process and you all deserve greatest appreciation for it. Thank you all."

The crowd cheered again with thunderous applause.

Lily then waved to the people and thanked them for their united stand. However, people just didn't want to disperse without saying "Hello" to Lily. So Lily stayed to acknowledge their affectionate feelings, steadfast backing and endorsement of the mission she had embarked upon.

One by one Lily met all of them and felt a great sense of achievement that the recall campaign was successfully accomplished and the Petition got submitted.

Samir was quietly happy seeing Lily blossom with radiance and joy.

By the time the meeting was over, a mild current of cool evening breeze had begun to sway and the sunset was turning the sky into a magnificently colorful covering. The panorama seemed so pleasant that Samir couldn't help recalling the days he spent at the lakeside with Lily. He knew that Lily so much enjoyed walking and running on the sandy shore and it was time again for a little fun, play and relaxation Samir thought. For life had been a bit hectic of late.

As the dusk began to fall and the moon began to rise, the lake looked all the more serene; the gentle sound of ripples adding a melodious touch to the air. It was a perfect setting for Samir and Lily to be together again in the quiet serenity of the sandy lakeshore.

Both of them needed it so much.

50

The Speaker presented the recall petition to the parliament and after verification of its authenticity, the parliament voted to accept it on the record.

Although some debate and procedural challenges were inevitable as expected, there was no recourse for those members whose constituents had overwhelmingly demanded their recall. They had to resign. And so they did.

The gun lobby was extremely upset over such an outcome and they were determined to somehow block reintroduction of the legislation in the parliament. They knew that Lily's re-election was now a foregone certainty and the candidates committed to supporting "Ban The Gun" legislation will fill the vacated seats. They suspected that Samir would also run this time from one of the vacated constituencies and easily win the seat. Hence, they viewed this as a fight for the survival of their industry and they were ready to play fair or foul, daring or dirty, clever or cruel, whatever it took to eliminate the adversary, an age-old practice of politics.

The ousted politicians were equally full of vengeance.

While the Election Commission was working on the re-election schedule, preparations for the cloned stem cell transplant were complete and Lily was required to get into the hospital for the procedure.

Although no reactions to the transplant were expected, nevertheless the physicians considered each transplant to be a unique situation and wanted to be fully prepared for any emergency. A large lumen triple port central line was, therefore, necessary for simultaneous infusion of blood, medication and other liquid preparations subsequent to transplant and to avoid necrosis by toxic drugs should the need for such infusions suddenly arise as a result of an adverse reaction consequent to the transplant.

To obviate unnecessary trauma, the central line was skillfully placed by an interventional radiologist under the upper chest wall into the jugular vein.

The transplant was scheduled for 8 a.m., so that an entire day was available for observation of the patient's response to the procedure.

Samir knew that the transplant team at the University was at the forefront and tops in the field, yet he was a bit troubled and anxious even though there was no cause for concern or any reason to worry. Perhaps the fear of the unknown superseded thoughtful analysis.

In any event, Samir got up early and arrived at Lily's bedside 7 a.m., before the mobile X-ray unit came in to take chest radiograms and the staff began attending to a pre-transplant protocol. Watching the elaborate preparations made Samir a bit nervous and he felt blank. Samir just couldn't think nor do anything else. He merely wanted to be with Lily. Deep down he had a strange empty feeling, a bit of unease.

The team of transplant physicians arrived on time, checked the lab reports, did a complete physical examination and finding all transplant protocols in order, signaled infusion of the cloned stem cells suspended in a buffered medium.

Samir kept watching the cells flow drip by drip into Lily's vein.

Lily did not manifest anything abnormal. She was calm without expressing any anxiety, just tightly holding Samir's hand with closed eyes as though that was all that she wished to hold on to in this world! Nothing else and only Samir seemed to be in her mind as the cells slowly dripped into her body.

Aware of the tense atmosphere prevailing in the room, the attending physician tried to initiate light conversation telling Lily: "Madam! After the transplant you would be so rejuvenated that you could take a gun and start shooting every parliamentarian who did not vote in favor of your legislation! Wouldn't that be miraculous?"

Everyone cracked up at the satire, breaking the prevailing tense atmosphere in Lily's room.

Lily couldn't help quipping back: "Might not be a bad idea, after all. What you sow is what you reap, isn't that the truth?"

Everyone poked fun and the jokes continued for a while, each adding to the conversation whatever came to mind, relevant or irrelevant!

The infusion of stem cells was complete in about 40 minutes but the administration of steroid was continued to avoid any unanticipated immune reaction to the transplant. Steroid was to be administered for three days and then tapered over the next three days. After observation of the patient over subsequent medication-free five days followed by evaluation of all lab and clinical tests confirming successful transplant of the cloned stem cells, the patient was ready to be discharged and followed routinely thereafter on an outpatient basis.

An enormous achievement of the molecularly designed targeted drug therapy and cloned stem cell transplant was that the patient did not get immunocompromised and the visitors, friends and the family could freely call on the patient while undergoing the procedure. Apart from this major medical advantage, visitations also helped to ameliorate the monotonous in-patient feeling. Flowers and get-well cards seemed to uplift her spirit and a cheerful feeling appeared to help early recovery.

News of the successful stem cell transplant spread with jubilation throughout the community and many a well-wisher including the Speaker of Parliament and the University President came in to see Lily at the hospital. Samir was elated at the genuine heart-felt feelings of the visitors and the dignitaries.

Friends, campaign staff and many others came to visit Lily at the hospital to express their joy at the triumphant remedy of the dreaded lymphoma and Lily was so happy to see them all.

Because of the unusual number of well wishers coming to visit Lily, the hospital was also quite lenient with the visiting hours.

Winter was usually mild around here but just the day before her scheduled discharge, the weather suddenly turned unusually cold. It became a cloudy, dark winter day and occasional snowflakes started falling. By the time the evening visiting-hours set in, however, the snow flurries had stopped and the ground was fairly clear. But the North Arctic wind was extremely crisp and not being used to such freezing cold, everyone who came in to see Lily had to put on some protective clothing such as a hat, an overcoat, a woolen scarf and mittens etc., to shield against the gust of northern chilly wind, which was mighty blustery.

Knowing full well that there was no security check at the hospital and finding the well awaited perfect opportunity, sparse traffic and only few people daring to head toward the hospital in the prevailing bitter cold, Tom, Steve, Neena and Phil dropped in as planned during the evening visiting hours around 8:20 p.m., in complete disguise as respectable visitors. While Neena and Tom engaged in pleasantries with Samir and Lily, appreciating both of them for their dedicated campaign and Lily's full recovery with cloned transplant, Steve and Phil cautiously surveyed the surroundings with their watchful eyes and finding 'all clear,' carefully reached their inner coat pocket gently pulling the silencer-fitted revolver and shot point blank at Lily and Samir. Both were killed instantaneously, all four of them then quietly leaving the hospital room in a normal manner so as not to raise any suspicion.

A revengefully planned, ruthless mission was meticulously accomplished.

It was not until the end of visiting hours and change of the night shift a little after 9 p.m., that the double murder was discovered by the attending nurse on her routine rounds. She was horrified seeing Samir and Lily's bodies slumped on the floor. Frightened, she rushed to report the ghastly scene to the authorities.

The hospital, town and the country were stunned in disbelief upon hearing the news and all kinds of leads, investigations and hunt for the perpetrators ensued as expeditiously as the bureaucratic system could pull together and coordinate various agencies.

Thousands gathered at the funeral to pay their last respect to this selfless intrepid young couple incredulously oblivious of repetitious human history!

Some cried and some found solace in the belief that even in death the parted souls were together!

But at eulogy no one had heart enough to muster any reason for this reality!

EPILOGUE

Despite intensive investigations, the police and detectives haven't yet been able to apprehend the perpetrators of the crime!